**"Not all women are attracted
to the type of man who
parades a—a brazen sexuality!"
Reva said, flaring.**

"The 'stud' type?" Drake suggested laconically.

"Yes, if you want to put it that way!"

He leaned across the table and traced the line of her jaw with a forefinger. The touch was like a moving thread of hot scarlet. Reva caught his hand to stop the erotic whisper of his fingertips against the vulnerable curve of her throat.

"You need a man you love heart and body and soul," he pursued with soft relentlessness.

"That—that's foolishness. Adolescent fantasy." She shook her head, trying to break the powerful spell. "Can't you get it through your head that I'm telling you no?" Reva demanded wildly. "I don't want to see you again."

"You're not attracted to me?"

"No!"

"Liar." He breathed the word on her as if it were a caress, not an epithet. She closed her eyes, reeling under the sensuous force of it. Then he smiled lazily, as if knowing he had branded her with the truth.

Dear Reader:

June 1983 marks SECOND CHANCE AT LOVE's second birthday—and we have good reason to celebrate! While romantic fiction has continued to grow, SECOND CHANCE AT LOVE has remained in the forefront as an innovative, top-selling romance series. In ever-increasing numbers you, the readers, continue to buy SECOND CHANCE AT LOVE, which you've come to know as the "butterfly books."

During the past two years we've received thousands of letters expressing your enthusiasm for SECOND CHANCE AT LOVE. In particular, many of you have asked: "What happens to the hero and heroine after they get married?"

As we attempted to answer that question, our thoughts led naturally to an exciting new concept—a line of romances based on married love. We're now proud to announce the creation of this new line, coming to you this fall, called TO HAVE AND TO HOLD.

There has never been a series of romances about marriage. As we did with SECOND CHANCE AT LOVE, we're breaking new ground, setting a new precedent. TO HAVE AND TO HOLD romances will be heartwarming, compelling love stories of marriages that remain exciting, adventurous, enriching and, above all, romantic. Each TO HAVE AND TO HOLD romance will bring you two people who love each other deeply. You'll see them struggle with challenges many married couples face. But no matter what happens, their love and commitment will see them through to a brighter future.

We're very enthusiastic about TO HAVE AND TO HOLD, and we hope you will be too. Watch for its arrival this fall. We will, of course, continue to publish six SECOND CHANCE AT LOVE romances every month in addition to our new series. We hope you'll read and enjoy them all!

Warm wishes,

*Ellen Edwards*

Ellen Edwards
SECOND CHANCE AT LOVE
The Berkley Publishing Group
200 Madison Avenue
New York, N.Y. 10016

# THE MARRYING KIND
## JOCELYN DAY

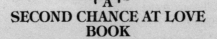

**SECOND CHANCE AT LOVE
BOOK**

THE MARRYING KIND

Second Chance at Love books are published by
The Berkley Publishing Group
200 Madison Avenue, New York, NY 10016

# Chapter One

REVA JONATHAN PEERED into the car window, one hand clinging to the door frame. "You'll call as soon as you get to San Jose?" she asked her son sitting in the back seat.

"Sure, Mom. I know the area code, and you have to put a *one* in front of it for long distance," eight-year-old Brian said importantly. "And I'll write to you, too."

"Don't worry if he doesn't call until late," Jill Anderson said soothingly. "We're going to take our time driving down the coast. And we'll drive *carefully*."

Reva smiled apologetically. "Drive carefully" was what she had been just about to say—again. But she knew Wally Anderson was a careful, competent driver or she would never have considered allowing Brian to ride all the way from the Oregon coast down to San Jose, California, with Wally and Jill.

"Reva Jonathan, you spend some time enjoying your freedom this summer," Jill admonished severely. "Don't just sit around and fuss and fret all the time."

Wally leaned across his wife to peer up at Reva. "Gloat about your victory over that development company," he advised, grinning. "Plan how you're going to spend your

1

self-made millions as the female cheese tycoon of Razor Bay."

"Spend a few wild weekends with Mark," Jill suggested. With an impish smile she added, "Better yet, spend a few weekends looking around to see what else is available."

Reva wrinkled her pert nose and ignored the affectionately teasing comments. She leaned into the car and gave Brian one last kiss. Reluctantly she released the door and waved until the car disappeared around the corner.

Reva blinked back a shimmer of tears as she walked into the house. In all Brian's eight years, she had never been separated from him for more than a weekend. And now he was gone for the entire summer. Perhaps she should never have agreed to let Bax have him for so long. Perhaps she shouldn't have agreed to let Bax have him at *all*. She knew Bax loved his son, of course, but so far he hadn't exactly proven himself the most reliable and responsible of fathers. Still, since Bax's remarriage, the child-support payments had arrived regularly, and he appeared to have settled into a permanent job with an insurance company. Perhaps he had finally matured out of that blithe let-tomorrow-take-care-of-itself attitude that Reva had found attractive as a teenager, much less so as a wife and mother. Bax's new wife had sounded pleasant and dependable on the phone. And Brian certainly needed to spend some time with his father. Every boy needed that.

Then a new thought struck Reva. What if Brian were so happy with his father and new stepmother that he didn't want to come home? What if—

*Stop that*, she commanded, exasperated with herself. She was already doing exactly what Jill had warned her not to do: fussing and fretting.

Briskly she gathered up the breakfast dishes and piled them in the sink. She glanced at her watch. Seven-thirty. She didn't have to be at the store for another hour. Oh, but today was the day the new sign was going up! She wanted to be sure and be there if the sign-company workers arrived early.

She showered, applied a minimal flick of makeup, and

slipped into trim-fitting navy-blue pants and a tailored cream blouse. She started toward the door, car keys in hand, then remembered she hadn't taken anything out of the freezer for dinner. She had the freezer door open, her hand on the usual package of hamburger, Brian's inevitable choice in food, when she suddenly remembered she would be eating alone tonight. She could have just a salad if she wanted. Or minestrone, which Brian hated. Or she could bring home a wedge of Brie and bottle of champagne and enjoy a deliciously decadent snack without once thinking she had to set a good meal-eating example for Brian!

For the first time she felt a small and quite unexpected ripple of anticipation toward the coming two months. As Jill had pointed out, she was temporarily free. Free to follow her own pursuits, free to live as she pleased without the twenty-four-hour-a-day responsibilities that went with motherhood. It gave her a breathlessly zesty feeling that something wonderful could happen, and brought more than the usual sparkle to her already lively hazel eyes.

Just as quickly, a heavy flood of guilt doused the flutter of anticipation. She was acting as if she was *glad* Brian was gone for the summer, and that absolutely was not true! She would miss him terribly. And she would worry about him.

Yet the delicious feeling of freedom, like a small, secret treasure, kept bubbling to the surface at unexpected moments during the day. She found herself making small but delightful plans while selling a block of smoked raw cheddar to tourists from Los Angeles. Yes, she definitely would dine on Brie and champagne tonight! And take an hour-long, uninterrupted bubble bath, and *not* turn on the kiddie television cartoons. While she waited for old Mrs. Coleman to decide between sharp cheddar and the new chocolate-flavored Neufchatel, she thought about spending a weekend in Portland. Not to conduct any business, not to do anything practical at all, just to enjoy herself shopping and sightseeing. Or she could run down to Ashland and take in a performance at the well-known Shakespearean theater. The possbilities were wide open!

Suddenly Reva realized Mrs. Coleman was speaking about

something other than cheese. "I'm sorry," Reva murmured guiltily. Time to get her feet back on solid earth. What she really needed to do with this summer's freedom was make some much needed changes in the store and get the business on its financial feet. "What were you saying?"

"I was saying I'm glad you didn't let that company get away with what they wanted to do with this building." Mrs. Coleman's voice was a bit testy. She was always saying young people these days didn't pay enough attention. "It would have been a shame to tear it down. My father served as mayor in this building when it was the city hall, you know."

Reva wrapped the cheese Mrs. Coleman had selected. Mrs. Coleman always deliberated a long time and then made exactly the same practical choice: a two-pound wedge cut from the big old-fashioned wheel of sharp cheddar. Reva hadn't known Mrs. Coleman's father had served as mayor in the building, though she had certainly dug up much other information in her research into the building's history in preparation for her presentation to the city council last week.

"I'm glad so many people agreed with me about preserving the building," Reva said. After Reva had spoken at the meeting, at least a dozen others had risen to echo her views. She handed the wrapped cheese to Mrs. Coleman. "I was afraid people might think it foolish to save the old building instead of having a modern shopping mall here."

Mrs. Coleman gave a snort of disdain. "There are lots of other places to put shopping malls, but there aren't any other old buildings in town like this one." She punctuated the point with emphatic little jabs of her head.

That was Reva's feeling exactly, though her interest in preserving the building was personal as well. If the building were torn down, she'd have to find a new location for her business. And she could afford neither the expense of moving to a new location nor the financial loss of not being able to do business during a relocation. Nor did she know of any suitable place where her business could be moved and still catch the tourist trade. At this point in Reva's delicately balanced business career, a forced move could have been disastrous.

The men from the sign company arrived far later than promised, but by closing time the new sign was in place. "Cheese 'n' Stuff," in bright, perky letters, now hung just beneath the marquee-type roof that extended from the building over the sidewalk. The sign was decorated at one end with a fat, smug-looking mouse nibbling a chunk of cheese. It replaced the staid, faded, "Quality Cheeses" sign that was lettered on the window, which couldn't even be seen by tourists over on Main Street. Reva was sure the new sign would help increase business. And she planned to advertise. Mrs. Parker, the former owner, hadn't advertised in years.

That evening, Reva carried out her bubble-bath, Brie, and champagne plans, adding a dreamy throb of background music from a seldom-used instrumental tape on the stereo. For an added touch of frivolous luxury, she recklessly tipped a dribble of champagne into the bath water.

She enjoyed the soothing, uninterrupted soak in the tub, relishing the luxury of the champagne and romantic music. But she was very much aware of a missing element in the setting she had created. Without a man, the music and champagne seemed just a little empty and pointless.

Ridiculous, she scolded herself. She didn't need a man to enjoy good music and fine champagne. Yet she couldn't escape a small, dreamy fantasy of a tall, handsome man striding arrogantly through the door, clinking wineglasses with her, his dark, smoldering eyes never leaving hers as he disrobed and slid boldly beneath the silky froth of bubbles . . .

Mark? she asked herself lightly.

No, Mark was away for the week, taking his daughter to visit grandparents in Seattle. But even if Mark were in town, Reva couldn't quite picture him striding arrogantly into her bathroom, much less envision him joining her in the tub with a glass of champagne. Not that Mark wasn't tall. Even good-looking, in a quiet, unobtrusive sort of way. But he was too . . .

*Stodgy* was the word that popped into her mind, but she quickly rejected it. *Sensible* was more accurate. Sensible and dependable. Exactly the qualities she wanted in a man as a father for Brian. Just because Mark Crossman was predictable and conservative didn't make him stodgy.

"Spend some wild weekends with Mark," Jill had said. Jill would no doubt be surprised, Reva thought wryly, if she knew Reva and Mark not only had never shared a wild weekend together, they had never even made love. Reva couldn't say for certain just why it had never happened. There really wasn't much opportunity, of course. The kids were always around, because she and Mark always planned activities that included them. Mark had made a few tentative moves toward making love, but Reva had put him off and he hadn't persisted. She was grateful for that, of course, and yet, perversely, occasionally annoyed by his consideration and understanding and lack of pressure. And then annoyed with herself for being femininely inconsistent and unreasonable.

She had also put off Mark's tentative discussions about getting married, though marriage was the obvious point toward which their relationship was drifting. Mark's daughter needed a mother, and Brian needed a strong, dependable father-in-residence. Brian was a good kid, yet Reva had noted uneasily what she feared were small danger signals in the way he sometimes withdrew in wary retreat from people. Marrying Mark would provide the foundation of solid emotional security Brian needed.

So what was she waiting for, she asked herself now as she trailed a cascade of iridescent bubbles idly through her fingers. Why had she so far avoided making a real commitment to Mark? Was she waiting for some strong, silent, masculine type to throw her down and ravish her? No, of course not. She wanted love and companionship as well as sexual attraction. If her former marriage was an accurate sample, sex was, in fact, highly overrated and fell far short of its wide publicity. And yet...

The telephone rang, and Reva leaped out of the tub to answer it, trailing bubbles and rivulets of water. It was

Brian, safe and sound at Bax's home in San Jose. After Brian chattered about the trip, Bax's new wife, Mikki, came on the line and assured Reva she was welcome to call any time she wanted to talk to Brian. Bax, Mikki explained a bit apologetically, wasn't home just then. It was his bowling night. Reva felt a surge of her old anger and frustration with Bax. Couldn't he have stayed home to greet his son after not seeing him for so long? She managed to argue down the anger. Bax couldn't have known what time Brian was arriving.

The next morning dawned beautifully clear and sunny, devoid of the misty fog that so often dominated the Oregon seacoast in summer. In appreciation, Reva slipped into a vivid, coral-colored sun dress instead of her usual outfit—practical tailored pants and blouse. She felt a surge of elation as she spied her bright new "Cheese 'n' Stuff" sign from a full block away.

Reva unlocked the door and opened the refrigerated cases to display the many varieties of cheese the store had to offer. She rearranged the Muenster and provolone chunks for better exposure and set out some postage-stamp-sized sample slices of the Monterey Jack cheese with jalapeño peppers. The teen-age girl who worked part-time arrived. A few customers drifted in and out, but it was not a particularly busy morning. That changed when the occupants of a chartered tour bus suddenly descended en masse on the shop. The out-of-state visitors were especially interested in the Oregan-made products, and Reva quickly sold an impressive amount of medium and sharp Tillamook cheddars and numerous bottles of Oregon specialty wines. She explained cheerfully, as she often did to curious tourists, that the town's name of Razor Bay came from the deliciously edible razor clams found around the nearby shores.

She was just wrapping a bottle of blueberry wine for a customer when she had the odd feeling that she was being watched. She glanced around. A man was standing just inside the open door, unsmiling, aloof from the crowd of jauntily dressed tourists milling around the store. Reva's first startled thought was that he would have fit quite nicely into her champagne-and-bubble-bath fantasy of last night. He was a few years older than her own twenty-seven years, with dark hair and eyes, boldly sculptured jaw and cheekbones, and a lean body that gave an impression of taut readiness in spite of his relaxed stance. At odds with the guarded, watchful expression in his eyes was a rakish mustache. He wore stylish, well-cut slacks and jacket and a pale blue dress shirt, but something about his lithely powerful build and bold masculinity transcended the expensive clothing. He had a certain indefinable air of sophistication and experience, but underneath was a hint of almost rough maleness. It was a devastating and disturbing combination. This man would never look ordinary, with or without the aid of well-cut clothes.

He acknowledged Reva's appraisal with a faint smile that held more mockery than warmth, and she felt a flush surge to the surface of her skin. She flushed partly from the realization that her look had been too thorough and lingering to be merely a clerk-and-customer glance—and he knew it. She also flushed because of her own unlikely mental processes. What was she doing imagining some man she had never before seen stepping naked into her bubble bath?

"Ma'am, you've forgotten to put my pear wine in the sack," a voice interrupted plaintively.

"Oh, yes, I did forget, didn't I?" Reva agreed, flustered. She jammed the bottle of wine hastily into the sack and went on to ring up the next sale.

The man made no move to purchase anything or to approach Reva, but she was disturbingly aware of his dark gaze following her every move. Finally the last of the tour-bus customers wandered out. Beth, her teen-age clerk, went to the back room to get a fresh stock of assorted crackers. The man sauntered casually toward the counter where Reva stood, obviously having waited until she was alone to approach her. The few lines of mature experience on his face enhanced rather than detracted from his sun-darkened good looks. Up close his dark hair had a hint of crisp curl.

"I'm sorry you had to wait. We're not usually so busy."

The small breathlessness in Reva's voice wasn't solely from the unexpected flurry of business. Her usually well-behaved heart was doing unfamiliar things in reaction to his interested appraisal. His gaze, though not so bold as to be actually objectionable, was hardly timid.

"I'm in no hurry," he said, obliquely confirming her thought that he had deliberately waited until she was alone. The probing gaze didn't strip her, but it was certainly exploratory.

"May I help you find something? We have some excellent new Danish cream Havarti. And we also carry cans of locally smoked salmon now." She named the products even though so far he had shown no interest in the store's wares.

"Sounds interesting," he said, agreeing noncommitally. He picked up a prepackaged wedge of Roquefort, but she had the impression he wasn't really looking at it. He had a well-kept but strong and thoroughly competent-looking hand, nothing soft or uncertain about it. "Nice little place you have here. Has it been here long? I don't recall seeing it the last time I was in Razor Bay."

That told Reva two things, one of which she had been almost certain already. He wasn't a local—or she'd surely have noticed him before in a town the size of Razor Bay. And he'd been here before. She wondered if he came often. She found herself attracted by his dark good looks and superior self-assurance, yet wary of those same characteristics. Though he had done nothing particularly assertive or aggressive, his male presence dominated the small store. She felt a flicker of annoyance. This was *her* store.

"The store has been here for years. Practically unnoticed, I'm afraid. I plan to change that now that I'm the owner," she added determinedly.

"A fairly recent business acquisition?"

Reva nodded. "I've worked here for several years, but I just bought the business a few days ago. My new sign just went up yesterday." She pointed with a certain pride to the jaunty new sign overhanging the sidewalk. She did not add that going into debt to buy the business and striking out on her own was both exciting and frightening.

"Very nice," he murmured. "You're planning other improvements?"

"There are a number of other things I hope to do with the store," Reva admitted.

"Such as?" He dropped the Roquefort and picked up a wedge of Brie, which made Reva remember, uncomfortably, her party the night before—and the thoughts that had flashed through her mind when she had first seen the stranger.

"I'd like to offer gift packs, ready for mailing," she continued. "Add a line of myrtlewood gift items, such as bowls and salad sets. Increase the supply and variety of wines. Perhaps set up a few tables and offer deli-style sandwiches. Buy some new refrigerated display cases. And have a large enough volume of business to be able to make larger, more economical purchases, of course." She suddenly felt a little self-conscious, revealing so much to a stranger. Why should he care? Yet he seemed interested.

"Sounds very ambitious." He glanced around, looking up at the old-fashioned high ceilings. "Perhaps this location is too small and you'll need larger quarters."

"Perhaps. The rooms next door are vacant, and I probably could expand into them. I like the old-fashioned atmosphere of this building, though I wouldn't mind if the landlord spent a few dollars modernizing the heating and electrical systems." She eyed the overhanging light fixture that blew bulbs with monotonous regularity.

"Are those systems unsafe?"

Something about the studied casualness of the question sent a warning flicker through Reva. Was he some kind of inspector out to make trouble for her? "Yes, quite safe," she said quickly.

"I'll take a box of those sesame crackers and a package of that shrimp and cream-cheese spread," the man said suddenly, as if he had noted a hesitancy in her voice and wanted to reassure her he was just an ordinary customer.

Reva was not convinced. There was nothing "ordinary" about him. He had a certain presence that went beyond the dark good looks and lithely powerful physique. "Do you come to Razor Bay frequently?" she asked with deliberate casualness as she rang up the sale.

"No." The flat, brusque statement definitely discouraged further questions. He added nothing to it.

"Well, you certainly hit a lucky day then. The weather is lovely," she said brightly, dropping the cash-register ticket in the sack with the cheese and crackers. "I heard on the local news that the fish are biting, too."

She was doing a bit of fishing herself, Reva acknowledged. Why was he in Razor Bay? Somehow he didn't look or act like the typical tourist or weekend fisherman. But her comment elicited no further information about his purpose there. He merely nodded in acknowledgment of her remark about fishing. She handed the sack to him, careful not to let her fingertips brush his. Odd, she thought. She couldn't recall ever before giving any thought to the possibility of that small contact between clerk and customer.

"Mrs. Jonathan, since we're not too busy right now, would it be all right if I run up to the post office for a minute?" Beth, her teen-aged clerk, interrupted with a touch on Reva's arm. "I've finished restocking the cracker shelf."

"Yes, that's fine. Pick up a roll of stamps for the store while you're there, would you please?" Reva requested. She punched the cash-register key and extracted a twenty-dollar bill. The tour-bus customers had left the outer door open, and Beth closed it as she went out.

Still the man made no move to leave. They both watched the door click shut as if it were an event of crucial importance. Reva felt flustered when their eyes swung to meet, as if it were a moment of secret tryst for which they had been waiting. She had been in the store with a lone male customer any number of times before, but never before had she been electrically aware of it as a man-woman situation.

"Was there something else you wanted?" she asked nervously. "May I help you find—"

"You could tell me if there's a *Mr.* Jonathan," he said, a faintly quizzical expression on his face. "I presume there is, yet I note the absence of a wedding ring . . ." His gaze drifted to her left hand, taking, Reva noted with a flush of indignation, a leisurely route over her bare shoulders and the ruffle of her sun dress that dipped a bit low in front. She resisted an urge to reach down and yank up the front of the dress.

"I don't think my marital status has any bearing on selling cheese and crackers!" she said. Her tart words were a protective barrier against the disturbing jolt of his meaningful remark and the bold journey of his eyes.

He smiled, a gleam of amusement in those dark eyes. "A beautiful woman affects sales of almost anything." He held up the sack. "Would you believe I don't even *like* cream cheese?"

"Then I'll take it back!"

"You haven't answered my question."

"Why—why do you want to know?"

"Because I'm not in the habit of asking some other man's wife to have lunch with me," he stated laconically.

"I—I usually just eat in the back room. I seldom leave the store." She took a steadying breath, then made a reckless leap, influenced by the speculative interest in his glance. "Actually, I'm not married now. I'm divorced."

"I see." His head was tilted, his gaze thoughtful. She had the feeling he was weighing something in his mind.

"And you?" she asked, challenging him when he continued to study her with that disconcertingly intense look.

He flashed her a brilliant smile, as if he had just come to a decision. "Blessedly single," he stated. "We'll make it dinner instead of lunch," he added decisively.

Reva retreated instantly. Attractive as this man was, she knew absolutely nothing about him, and she was suddenly wary, wishing she hadn't admitted quite so quickly to being divorced. He had obviously taken the statement as some sort of automatic acceptance of his invitation.

"I have other plans for tonight," she stated coolly.

"Another engagement?"

"No."

He leaned across the counter and ran lean, strong fingers through the short, sassy cap of chestnut curls that framed her face. Reva was too startled to pull away. Or was it that she *couldn't* pull away, that some instant electricity flowing between them riveted her to the spot? She felt the masculine warmth of his hand, and behind it the strength held in reserve. He tangled his fingers in the crisp chestnut mass, and the lively strands curled around his fingers as if embracing them.

"Wh—what are you doing?" she finally managed to ask as his fingertips tucked an independent curl behind her ear and lingered on the sensitive lobe.

"Checking out your hair. Isn't the old, 'I have to wash my hair tonight' line the excuse you planned to lay on me next?" Amusement twitched his strong mouth. "But you can't use that line," he added softly. "Your hair feels like clean silk."

He lifted a few strands and let them curl softly against her temple, seemingly fascinated. Reva was suddenly conscious of her bare shoulders exposed above the cotton sun dress, aware that his hand was sliding down her throat as his eyes held hers. She felt the pulse in her throat throb against the warm pressure of his thumb, and her breasts went taut, as if anticipating a further descent of the lazily prowling hand.

The tinkle of the bell on the opening door finally jolted her into outraged motion. How dare he touch her like that? And what was the matter with her, just standing there permitting his touch? She jerked back and ran nervous fingers through her hair to push it back into place. It felt strangely lush and voluptuous, as if his touch had wrought some sensuous change in it.

"You have a customer," he said smoothly, and then, significantly, "I'll wait."

The customer didn't take nearly long enough, to Reva's way of thinking. The woman picked up blue and cream cheeses, paid for them, and was out the door before Reva had time to reorganize the chaos in her mind—and not nearly enough time to erase the racing tingle from her skin.

When the customer was gone, the man lifted a dark eyebrow. "So, to take up where we left off, I'll pick you up for dinner. When and where?"

"I don't even know your name!" Reva replied distractedly. "And you don't know mine!"

"Yours is Reva Jonathan," he replied promptly. He gave her a small, slightly wicked grin and added, as if it were a special secret they shared, "Divorcée."

"I still don't know yours!"

"Drake McQuaid." He smiled again. "And Drake McQuaid is taking you to dinner. I'll pick you up at eight o'clock," he stated when she made no move to name a time. "Where do you live?"

"No! I mean—" Reva clamped her lower lip between her teeth. Just what did she mean? There was no reason she *couldn't* have dinner with Drake McQuaid. She didn't have to worry about finding someone to stay with Brian. Even though neither she nor Mark had been seeing anyone else, there were no promises or commitments between them. Their exclusive relationship was more accidental than purposeful. Yet it wasn't really thoughts of Mark that held her back. There was an unknown quantity to Drake McQuaid. He was too attractive, too forceful, too sure of himself. His brief touch on her hair and throat had held an electric intimacy. His lazy, amused smile tugged at something dormant deep inside her, stirred something she wasn't sure she wanted awakened. An unknown danger hovered around Drake McQuaid, a danger that unexpectedly had a tantalizing sizzle of excitement.

"You haven't got another date," he pointed out reasonably as Reva continued to hesitate. "We've already established the fact that your hair doesn't need washing. And surely you have to eat, don't you?"

Reva's lower lip was still trembling, but now it wavered between nerves and laughter. There was something delightfully audacious about his walking in here, guessing that she had been about to say she planned to wash her hair tonight, and then arrogantly telling her he was taking her to dinner. She felt oddly off-balance, as if he were always a step ahead of her.

"I suppose I am curious about one thing, however," he

added on a speculative note as she continued to vacillate between no and yes.

"What's that?"

"How come a beautiful woman like you *doesn't* have another date on a summer Saturday night?"

"Actually, I—I don't date much." He raised an eyebrow, as if skeptical of that, but it was more or less true. The casual outings and evenings she and Mark spent together with the kids couldn't really be called dates. "I have an eight-year-old son. But he's spending the summer in California with his father."

"Then there is absolutely no reason you can't have dinner with me," Drake McQuaid pronounced decisively.

No reason at all, she echoed to herself. She was temporarily free as a bird. So why not fly with that freedom, she asked herself recklessly. He wasn't asking her to make some lifetime commitment, just to share an evening, an evening that held the deliciously tantalizing appeal of the unknown.

"Well?" he prompted.

She felt oddly . . . virginal. Which was ridiculous, of course. She with an eight-year-old son! But the breathless feeling was there, as if she'd just been asked for her very first date.

Yet some small bit of down-to-earth caution made her add a qualification to her sudden, rash decision to accept the invitation from this darkly handsome stranger with the flashing eyes. "Perhaps I could meet you somewhere." In that case, if Drake McQuaid turned out to have ten hands and bedroom ideas, she could simply slip away in her car and disappear. She wouldn't be stuck somewhere, having to depend on him to get her home.

Her thinking, she realized from the amused gleam in those dark eyes, was as obvious as if she'd handed him a typed message. But he didn't appear to object.

"Fine. Eight o'clock. In the lounge at the Inn of the Shaman Mask. The Sea Lion Room, I believe it's called."

She concealed a small jolt of surprise. The inn was the

most elegant and expensive motel-restaurant complex on this stretch of the Oregon coast, named for its impressive collection of carved Northwest Indian masks. It attracted guests from all over the country and was out of the financial range of most of Reva's and Mark's friends, except for very special occasions.

As Drake headed toward the door, he tossed a smile and yet another audacious comment over his shoulder to her. "And wear something that shows off those gorgeous shoulders of yours."

# Chapter Two

OF ALL THE NERVE, Reva thought indignantly. Telling her what to wear! But it just so happened that the most attractive dress in her limited wardrobe did leave her shoulders bare. She assured herself that she wore the dress, a clingy white crepe with little diamond shimmers of satin in the fabric, because it really was the only dress she owned that was dressy enough for the Inn of the Shaman Mask, not because of Drake's insolent command to bare her shoulders. To prove that, she covered the expanse of bare skin with a lacy shawl before driving up the coast to the inn.

The inn was built on a windswept point overlooking the ocean. It was an irregularly shaped yet elegantly proportioned structure, with soaring, sharply angled roof lines that formed an imposing silhouette against the mist drifting up from the wave-washed rocks below. The weathered cedar-and-rock structure fit into the rugged coastal setting but was neither dwarfed nor overwhelmed by it. Setting and structure complemented rather than competed with each other. The golf course stretched like a sinuous green-velvet blanket among jumbled ravines and massive boulders. Drake McQuaid, Reva thought a bit tremulously, couldn't have chosen a setting that better matched the natural dominance of his own forceful personality.

In spite of having lived in the area most of her life, Reva had not been in the inn more than a half-dozen times, and each of those marked some special occasion. Was this a special occasion? Her heart gave an erratic flutter of response to the question, but she calmed it with a warning that what felt special to her was no doubt just a minor incident to Drake McQuaid. Somehow he had the ability to make her feel like a starry-eyed adolescent instead of a sensible mother and businesswoman. She must not let herself get carried away by this temporary flirtation with freedom.

Reva paused at the top of the broad, plushly carpeted steps leading down to the stone-arched doorway of the lounge. Except for a mirrored glitter behind the bar, the lounge looked dim and intimate. She jumped nervously when a hand touched her elbow. Drake had evidently been standing to one side waiting for her. He looked smoothly urbane in charcoal suit, French-cuffed white shirt, and heavy silk tie, but that dark mustache and brilliant flash of smile overlaid the sophistication with a certain air of reckless dash and fire.

"You—startled me!"

"Sorry. I paused for a moment to think how fortunate I was that such a lovely woman was looking for me." He smiled again and slipped his hand under the shawl. He guided her with easy assurance into the lower-level lounge. "We'll have a drink before dinner. Our table in the dining room won't be ready for a few minutes."

The lounge was busy but not crowded. Several small spotlights accented the large, ferocious-looking Indian masks for which the inn was famous. The figure of a carved wooden sea lion dominated one subtly lit corner.

"Are you staying here at the inn?" Reva asked after they were seated at a tiny table lit with a brass lantern.

"Temporarily. What would you like to drink?"

Reva asked for white wine rather than a mixed drink. She studied Drake surreptitiously while he placed the orders.

He hadn't exactly evaded her question, but she had the feeling he had brushed it aside, as if he preferred not to talk about himself.

Was he married, she wondered with an uneasy jolt. He'd said he wasn't, but that didn't prove anything, of course. A married man on the prowl didn't go around announcing his married state. His tanned left hand showed no telltale evidence of a ring, but that didn't prove anything either. Not that she was eyeing him as a potential marriage partner, of course. She simply did not go out with married men.

"You seem a little tense," he observed as they waited for the drinks. "Busy day at the store?"

"Off and on. You really may return the cream-cheese spread if you bought it just because..." Her offer trailed off awkwardly because she wasn't sure why he had bought the spread if he didn't like cream cheese.

"Because I was bewitched into buying it by a pair of dancing hazel eyes and a pixie smile?" He smiled at her discomfort. She was uncertain if he was complimenting or teasing her. "Actually, I had some for a snack this afternoon, and it was delicious."

Their drinks arrived, and it was a relief for Reva to have something to do with her nervous hands. She clasped the tulip bowl of the wineglass as if it were a lifeline. There were a dozen questions she wanted to ask him, yet everything sounded too prying and personal, as if she were sizing him up for marriage eligibility. And there was a certain indefinable air about him that proclaimed arrogantly he was not the marrying kind. She had no trouble at all bantering or making idle chitchat with customers in the store, and she could handle aggressive salesmen with brisk efficiency, but the plush setting and Drake's dark good looks and easy poise seemed to have drained away whatever hard-won sophistication she possessed.

"Are you just visiting here in Oregon?" she finally managed to ask casually.

"Don't tell me I look like a Californian!" He pretended a mock horror.

Reva laughed, but again she was aware of a vague feeling

that he had detoured her question.

Suddenly Drake leaned forward, his dark eyes intent on hers. "I admire you very much, do you know that?" he said unexpectedly.

Reva's hazel eyes widened in return. "You do?" The words came out sounding as astonished as she felt. Again she had that feeling of being kept off-balance by him, that his thought processes moved more quickly than hers, though she had never been accused of being slow. "I mean . . . thank you."

Then a dark suspicion grated on her as she felt his gaze slip to the shoftly shadowed valley in the halter neckline of her dress. "Just what is it you admire, Mr. McQuaid?" she asked. "My IQ exceeds my bust measurement, if you're interested in numbers." Reva was well aware that her trim figure, though neatly proportioned, was neither elegantly model-slim nor lushly voluptuous.

He lifted a dark eyebrow, unperturbed that his wandering gaze had been impaled. "Can't a man admire both?" he asked innocently. He leaned back, the lazy rove of his eyes undeterred by her tart comment. "Actually, I'd say you're quite nicely endowed in both those areas, but at the moment I was expressing admiration for something else."

She was still suspicious of him but too curious not to ask, "And what is that?"

"I don't know much about you, but I know it can't be easy for a young, divorced mother, raising a child more or less alone, to take on the risks and responsibilities of buying and running a business of her own. I admire anyone who stands on his, or her, own two feet and challenges the world."

"I—I don't know that I'm challenging the world," Reva admitted, feeling a pleased glow under his unexpected praise, "but I do know I want very much to make a success of the store. And still be a good mother to Brian, of course."

"How long have you been divorced?"

"About three years. But this summer is the first time Brian has spent any time with his father." It was the first time Bax had landed in one place long enough for a visit to be possible, Reva added wryly to herself.

"How long were you married?"

"About six years. We married right out of high school. Which was one of our mistakes, I suppose. We both had a lot of growing up to do."

Drake took a sip of his drink. He swirled the dark amber liquid thoughtfully, making the hollow ice cubes clink and glitter in the glow of mellow light. "You think it might have worked if you'd waited until both of you were older?"

It was an unanswerable question, of course, but one Reva had pondered many times. The question she had in exasperation asked herself more often *during* the marriage, however, was, wasn't Bax *ever* going to grow up? It was she who had to cope with bill collectors, hassle with the insurance company when Bax wrecked the car, fib to the plywood mill when the foreman called to find out why Bax hadn't been to work for two days. At the time, of course, she had no idea he hadn't been to work, much less why. When she had confronted him that evening, he had just shrugged and said the Chinook salmon were biting and he felt like fishing instead of being cooped up in the mill.

Yet Bax had protested the occasional temporary jobs she took to help out when family finances got particularly precarious, evidently feeling his manhood was somehow threatened. He had also resented the occasional courses she took at the local community college for the same reasons, as if afraid she might rise above him.

She couldn't say just when she had fallen out of love with Bax. It was a gradual process. Before marriage, his carefree attitude had seemed attractively independent and unconventional, interestingly unfettered, but later she'd thought in frustration that it often seemed as if she had not one but *two* boys to raise. And she didn't like playing the role of mommy to the one she had married. Bax had acted hurt and bewildered when she first said she wanted a divorce, and it took all her strength not to weaken. But his period of mourning—if it could be called that—was brief. He leaped enthusiastically into a mobile, single lifestyle, working a few months here, quitting to dash to something else, and moving from woman to woman with equal frequency. She did not, Reva thought fervently, envy Mikki.

After Bax's erratic irresponsibility, Mark's solid reliability was a soothing relief, like going from storm-tossed waves into the calm of a tranquil bay. If Mark told his own daughter, Jade, and Brian that he was going to take them somewhere, he did it. He kept his bills paid. Of course, Mark hadn't been too calm when she decided to buy the store. He would have preferred that she marry him.

"Was that a difficult question?" Drake asked lightly. "It doesn't seem easy for you to answer."

Reva smiled quickly, a little apologetically. "I'm sorry. I was just thinking." She had always been careful to keep her frustration and exasperation with Bax to herself. She thought a good opinion of Brian's father was important for the boy's own self-esteem.

The dining-room hostess arrived to tell them their table was ready. On their way out of the lounge, two very attractive young women, somewhat younger than Reva, smiled and said very flirty hellos to Drake. He smiled back but didn't pause for introductions.

Their table was in an excellent location next to the enormous window overlooking the jagged rocks and crashing waves below. The rocks were now almost obscured by darkness and drifting mist, and a foggy grayness had swallowed up the horizon. The fog swirling against the window lent an enclosed intimacy to the big dining room, an intimacy that was enhanced by the golden pool of flickering candlelight that took in no more than their table.

Drake held the chair for her. When she was seated, his hands slipped the lacy shawl deftly from her shoulders. She tried to hold on to it, but he removed it firmly, his fingertips lingering ever so lightly on her bare skin.

"I like a pleasant view when I eat," he remarked. He sat down across from her, and his gaze approvingly roamed the creamy curve of her shoulders and the pearly flush of her skin. "And this view is very pleasant indeed." The candlelight danced in his eyes, or perhaps it wasn't the candlelight but a certain dancing deviltry of his own . . .

A shiver tingled through Reva, prickly but strangely delicious, like the thrill of excitement before starting a wild roller-coaster ride. Was she poised at the top of just such a ride, she wondered, feeling a sudden sense of panic as she looked at Drake, so darkly handsome, so sure of himself.

"Are you cold?" His voice sounded contrite, as if perhaps he blamed himself for her chill because he had removed her shawl.

"No. I—I guess the fog just looks cold," she said lamely. The shiver had come from something else entirely, something she couldn't begin to explain. And wouldn't explain if she could, she thought with a small flame of embarrassment at the decidedly erotic tingle. Her palms felt damp and her breasts rigid, and there was a tightening somewhere deep and intimate inside her. What next, she wondered, furious with herself. Just because she was in the presence of a good-looking, virile, well-dressed man who was obviously at ease in these expensive surroundings was no reason for her body to react as if she were some sex-starved divorcée. Mark didn't affect her that way.

Briskly she selected fresh filet of salmon à l'anglaise from the cosmopolitan menu. She declined another glass of wine. Setting the sleek golden menu aside, she sat up very straight in her chair. "I believe we got sidetracked. You never did tell me if you're visiting here in Oregon or . . . ?" She deliberately left the question dangling so he would have to provide an answer. She did not intend to let him take another evasive sidestep. At this point she still knew no more than his name and the fact that he was—supposedly— unmarried.

"I live in Portland, more or less. I keep an apartment and office and collect my mail there, but I'm traveling on business around the state much of the time. I really like the coast better than Portland, and I've considered moving over here. Were you born and raised here?"

"I was born in the San Francisco Bay area, but my family moved here when I was only four." As smoothly as that, Reva realized later, he had swung the conversation back to her. The realization did not come, however, until after she had told him about her growing-up years on the coast, her brother's death in a navy accident, and her parents' move to Minnesota. That had come shortly after Reva's marriage, when her father received a forest-service promotion. Drake was very good at asking encouraging, leading questions, she realized.

His interest was flattering, she thought as the waiter removed the dinner plates, but her talkativeness left her feeling faintly uneasy. She couldn't put her finger on any particular bit of information she should not have revealed to Drake, but she had the definite feeling that she had talked too much, something quite uncharacteristic of her. He, obviously, had a supreme ability to be deftly closemouthed. She was determined to turn the tables on him, but before she had the opportunity, a female voice interrupted.

"Reva!"

Reva looked up into the astonished face of Ann Hamilton. Ann's husband, Howard, was an English teacher at the same junior high where Mark taught math.

"Ann—and Howard! How nice to see you," Reva said brightly. She made awkward introductions, aware of Ann's burning curiosity about the man with Reva—aware, too, that Mark would hear practically the moment he got back to town that she had been seen at the inn with some strange man. Not that she'd intended to keep it a secret from Mark, of course, but she'd planned to tell him in her own way. She had not expected to run into anyone she knew here.

"We're going to go down and dance the night away," Ann said gaily. "I figure we ought to be able to do that at least once a year."

"Is it your anniversary?" Reva asked.

Ann nodded. "The tenth. Isn't that incredible?"

"Congratulations. I hope you have many more."

"Why don't you join us later?" Ann suggested. "I hear the music is terrific. Some group direct from a casino at Lake Tahoe."

Reva hesitated. She liked the Hamiltons, but they were really Mark's friends more than hers, and their conversation at social events inevitably dragged back to school gossip, school budgets, and the gross underpayment of teachers.

"We'll think about it," Drake cut in smoothly, rescuing Reva and at the same time dazzling Ann with a brilliant smile. "Thanks for the invitation."

Reva expected Drake to be curious about the Hamiltons, but he chose instead to talk about the seals he had seen frolicking in the surf on a beach walk he had taken earlier that evening.

They finished the creamy-rich amaretto mousse-cake dessert and coffee. Drake looked at her inquiringly.

"Would you like to join your friends and dance for a while?" he asked.

"Actually, they're more like—friends of a friend," she said evasively.

He considered that. "A male friend?"

"Yes."

His expression didn't change, except for a slight narrowing of the eyes. "A very *close* male friend?"

"In some ways." Reva evaded again.

"And where is this close friend tonight?" The question held just a hint of mocking challenge.

"He's out of town," Reva admitted reluctantly. She hated the way it made her sound as if she were sneaking around behind Mark's back.

Drake eyed her a moment longer, his brow marked with a line that was almost a scowl. Then he dismissed Mark with a shrug and another dazzling smile. "How lucky for me that I chose this day to walk into your store then." He stood up. "Now, would you care to go down and dance? Or, the inn has a marvelous heated pool and jacuzzi..."

"Actually, I think I'd just like a little fresh air. I often walk on the beach for a few minutes in the evening."

He wrapped the soft shawl around her shoulders. "Alone?" His hands lingered as he stood behind her. She could feel a reserve of male strength flowing through the light touch, and his breath fanned a trail of warmth on her neck as he leaned forward for her answer.

She heard what sounded like a hint of accusation in the single word, perhaps because she occasionally felt guilty slipping off for a few minutes without Brian. "Sometimes Brian comes along," she said defensively.

"I was thinking more of your 'close friend.'"

"He doesn't care for the beach."

Mark had been raised in the Midwest and moved to Razor Bay to teach only because the coastal air alleviated some of the allergies his daughter suffered in Illinois. He admitted Oregon's rugged coastline was awe-inspiring, but he wasn't wild about personal contact with it. The pieces of graceful, silvered driftwood that captured Reva's imagination appealed to Mark only as a practical source of wood for his fireplace. She had once found and hauled home a rare chunk of myrtlewood, intending to cut and polish it into bookends, later to find Mark had tossed it on the backyard barbecue to cook hamburgers for the kids.

"But he has many other admirable qualities," she said in an argumentative tone, as if Drake had made some derogatory remark about Mark.

"I'm sure he has," Drake agreed smoothly, though his faintly condescending smile somehow contradicted his agreeable words.

He put his arm around her shoulders as they went out the heavy glass doors to the deck. The wind had lulled to a mere whisper, which swirled the mist like a silvery veil over the wooden railing. Reva felt droplets instantly bead her skin and hair. The damp air had a clean, fresh scent, as if it had just been newly created somewhere out there on the foggy edges of eternity. The waves crashing into the rocks below were invisible now, but their sound seemed amplified by the drifting mist. At first the sound was a solid roar, but then Reva could pick out separate undertones of attack and retreat. She listened with lips parted, still fascinated with the sights and sounds and scents of the sea, even though she had lived almost a lifetime within their influence.

Mark thought the endless crash of the waves a bit melancholy, sometimes even annoyingly noisy, but to Reva it was a reassuring sound, something timelessly unchanging in a world that often seemed to move and change with dismaying swiftness.

"Your eyes are shining," Drake said softly.

They walked along the weathered railing until they reached the farthermost end of the deck. Here the mist felt heavier, as if spray from the waves below rose to mingle with it. They were the only strollers on the deck on this cool, damp night. Reva leaned against the wooden rail, head thrown back to catch the raw scent of ocean and mist. Ahead, the gray-white mass looked thick and impenetrable, but it was a shallow, shifting layer of fog, and a sudden drift let moonlight shimmer through, bathing them in a misty, silver radiance. The strange, diffused light emphasized the angular line of Drake's jaw and the dark hollows of his eyes, giving him a forbiddingly brooding expression. He looked darkly aristocratic, as if in another time or life he might have ruled as lord of some baronial mansion that humbled even the massive elegance of the inn.

"What are you thinking?" he asked, catching her bemused expression.

"That this all seems a little unreal . . ."

"Unreal?" He tilted his head to study her.

"Like some fairy tale I made up in my mind. Tall, dark, handsome stranger walks into my store, sweeps me off my feet, carries me off to his castle among the crags and mists . . ." She laughed self-consciously.

He laughed, too, a rich, intimate sound. "As I recall, you were rather insistent upon driving to the 'castle' yourself, so you could make a hasty retreat, if necessary."

She laughed again, still self-conscious. As she suspected, he had fully recognized what she was doing.

Then the laughter ceased as Drake turned her into his arms with a masterful, deliberate sureness. "Does this seem unreal?"

He dipped his head to hers, and her face lifted without protest. It was a moment meant for a kiss, a magical heartbeat in time that would have been incomplete without a kiss in the misty moonlight.

Droplets of mist touched her upturned face with dewy moistness, and the diffused moonlight caressed her closed eyelids. With his hands on her waist, his mouth took hers with an infinite sweetness, enveloping it in tender warmth. Her arms rose to encircle his neck, and the shawl fell unheeded to the wooden deck. Her lips parted beneath the commanding pressure of his, but he made no move to instantly invade their opening warmth. He unhurriedly moved his lips against hers, tasting their sweetness and learning their curved softness. His tongue traced the outline of her mouth as if it were a newly discovered treasure to be mapped and charted before undertaking a more complete exploration. She felt the strong length of his lithely muscled body, and she was sharply aware of his solid maleness beneath the expensive suit. The mustache felt crisp and ticklish against her skin, unfamiliar but pleasant.

His mouth twitched when he lifted his lips from hers. "Don't tell me this is the first time you've ever been kissed by a man with a mustache," he said teasingly.

"Well, actually—it is," she admitted.

"How do you like it?"

"I'm not sure yet." Her hazel eyes danced, teasing him back. "Maybe you'll have to show me again."

He framed her face with his hands and complied. The unhurried kiss was teasing at first, emphasizing the feel of his mustache against her skin. But the lingering kiss deepened, hinting at a passion rising on some far horizon. A shiver of mingled pleasure, danger, and delicious anticipation shivered through her. With no thought for the consequences, Reva took an eager step that brought her into closer intimacy with the maleness of his body, and it was she who injected a certain reckless urgency and need into the teasing kiss. Her arms tightened almost fiercely around his neck, crushing her breasts against his chest, and her tongue found the sweet warmth of his mouth.

He lifted his head and gazed down at her, and she was surprised and a little taken aback to see that the earlier, darkly brooding expression on his face had returned. He looked almost as if he resented her for inserting an erotic sensuality into the kiss and forcing him to acknowledge his own male arousal. The passion on that shadowy horizon had leaped into the sharp focus of *now*.

Reva's lips parted in dismay. She felt suddenly humiliated, as if she had overstepped some invisible boundary of propriety. Perhaps she had overstepped, she realized, stunned and a little shocked at herself. What had come over her to act so forward, so blatantly eager?

With a small cry, she tried to wrest herself out of his grasp, puzzled by this strange combination of held-back desire and angry resentment in him. For a moment his grip relaxed, but then it clamped down again, harder and harsher than before. His arms wrapped around her and crushed her to him, molding each inch of their bodies together in unrestrained intimacy. His kiss was deep and hungry and thrusting. Where before he had approached her mouth as if it were some fragile treasure to be teased and explored, now he plundered the treasure with arrogant abandon. His tongue invaded the warm recesses of her mouth while the hard outlines of his body imprinted themselves on the softly feminine hollows of hers. One hand laced her bare back with rough-velvet caresses and then descended to explore the firm curves below with arrogant possession.

She angrily resisted the sudden change in him, at the same time berating herself for having invited it—and paradoxically fighting an unwanted flood of raw desire within herself. It was unfamiliar and shocking in its power. She wanted to battle and claw not away from him but ever closer to his sinewy male strength. She wanted to explore and be explored, give and receive, satisfy and be satisfied. She felt a fierce, sharp demand from within her own body and the answering demand in his.

"Let go of me!" she demanded, fighting herself as well as him. Her words were broken by short gasps for breath as she struggled against the harsh bands of his arms. Her hair was in her eye, her dress twisted awry.

He forced her back against the railing and held her there. "You started this," he pointed out with deadly accuracy. "When a woman kisses a man the way you just did, I think

it's safe to assume she has more in mind than holding hands.'"
A lock of dark hair fell toward his eyes and he was breathing
rapidly, but his words, in sharp contrast to her jerky gasps,
came out evenly.

"I don't want to hold hands or—or anything with you!"
she said breathlessly. Her back was arched over the railing,
and the sharp angle of the wooden rail cut into her soft flesh.

He suddenly became aware of that. He stepped back and
she straightened, relieving the painful pressure against her
back.

"I'm sorry," he said stiffly. "I didn't mean to hurt you."

The halter neckline of her dress had been shoved so far
to one side that the rosy circle around the peak of her breast
was exposed. Self-consciously, Reva straightened the dress,
aware of an almost painful sensitivity in her breasts as the
material slid across the rigid tips. The fog had shifted, and
at the moment Drake and Reva stood in a hard, metallic
blaze of moonlight.

"If you'll excuse me . . ." She kept her head high and
fixed a frosty expression on her face and a coolness in her
voice, looking deliberately through rather than at him.

"No." He grabbed her arm, not gently. "I want to talk
to you." In the moonlight his hard expression was a sculptured composition of silver and shadow.

"You've had all evening to talk," Reva said aloofly.
"Evidently you had other things on your mind."

"I had the impression your thoughts wandered a bit also,"
he retorted with a certain grim humor.

"Thank you for a lovely dinner." Reva kept her voice
coolly formal, refusing to acknowledge that only moments
before her blood had raced with a wildfire of passion inappropriate to the time and place.

"You can cut the aloof formality," Drake said bluntly,
slicing through the frosty wall she had tried to erect around
herself. "I feel we already know each other a little too
intimately for that." His gaze dropped deliberately to her
breasts, where the cold cut of moonlight distinctly revealed
the shape of her nipples straining against the clinging fabric.

Her body felt marked by the hard imprint of his male desire, branded by the heat of him.

"I don't know anything about you!" she protested wildly. The brief flare of passion between them meant nothing in the realm of true intimacy.

The twist of his mouth might have been an acknowledging smile. "I'm planning to correct that."

She swallowed and crossed her arms over her breasts. "Very well, I'm listening."

"You're cold," he observed suddenly.

Yes. Her skin prickled with actual chill this time, and an involuntary shiver shuddered through her. She clutched her hands against her bare arms, trying to stop another shiver.

Where's your shawl?" He glanced around, spotted the froth of fabric lying on the deck, and bent to retrieve it. As if by prearranged design, a lift of breeze drifted it lazily out of his grasp. He reached for it again, and again the erratic breeze teased it away. It clung to the railing for a moment, and then, like a giant moth, floated gently into the foggy nothingness.

"I'll replace it," Drake said as it disappeared into the unseen crash of waves below them.

"That won't be necessary."

She truly was cold now, shivering almost uncontrollably. She clenched her teeth together to keep them from chattering.

"I'm still going to talk to you," he warned. "We'll go inside."

He put his arm around her bare shoulders. She resisted for a moment, then, with stiff reserve, accepted the welcome warmth of his body. They moved to the glass doors.

He pulled the door open. "We'll go to my room," he said decisively.

"No, we won't," Reva countered, just as decisively.

He glanced at her, the dark scowl on his face giving way to a wry twist of humor. "Perhaps you're right," he agreed. "We might never get around to talking. But later . . ."

The smile turned lazily meaningful, but Reva determinedly ignored it. She didn't let herself comtemplate "later."

"A drink in the lounge then?" he suggested.

Reva was not about to have her wits befuddled by a drink, given his deft ability to deflect a conversation away from himself. "Doesn't the inn have a coffee shop?"

"It might not be open at this hour."

"We can check."

He gave her a small smile, acknowledging she had won this little round.

One small section of the coffee shop was open, although it was deserted except for a couple of men drinking coffee at the counter. Reva and Drake sat in a padded booth, and Drake ordered two coffees from the waitress. Reva pushed nervous fingers through her hair and uneasily gave her dress a surreptitious glance to make sure everything was decently covered. Her chill was gone by now, but she felt loose and disorganized, not at all her usual, crisply efficient self.

"So, what do you want to know about me?" Drake asked conversationally.

Reva took a shaky breath. At the risk of sounding unsophisticated or narrow-minded, or even like some man-hungry divorcée with a one-track mind, she was determined to find out one thing.

"Are you married?"

"I told you I wasn't." He sounded mildly annoyed, as if he had expected a higher class of question from her. "Do I somehow look or act married?"

"No," she answered shortly. If anything, he had a distinctly unmarried air about him. "But I suppose that's what makes some married men so dangerous. They don't look married. And certainly don't act married."

"Do you think I'm dangerous?" His expression was quizzically amused.

"You're evading the qestion," she retorted, fully aware that she was evading *his* question.

"No, I am not married," he said flatly, as if it were a bothersome subject he preferred to get out of the way. "I was once, but it didn't last long. I've been divorced for

seven or eight years. No children," he added, as if he suspected that would be her next question.

The coffee arrived. Reva added cream to hers. Drake
left his black. She glanced at him obliquely out of the corner
of her eye. His eagerness to talk seemed to have dwindled.
He stirred the black coffee, his expression preoccupied,
almost frowning.

Another man walked into the coffee shop and started
toward the men at the counter. Then he glanced at Drake
and Reva in the booth and unexpectedly detoured toward
them.

"McQuaid," the big man boomed. He was expensively
dressed, but somehow the clothes looked out of place on
him. His beefy body seemed to bulge out of collar and
sleeves.

Drake glanced up. His eyes narrowed, as if it took him
a moment to place the man. Then he dredged up a name.
"Wheeler," he acknowledged with a slight nod.

"I hear your little plan got shot down by the city council
the other night." Wheeler grinned. "Tough luck. Between
the environmentalists and the no-growthers and some hysterical broad protecting a tumbledown old building as if
it were her virginity, it's damned hard to do anything these
days. Right?"

It took Reva a shocked moment to realize *she* was that
"hysterical broad." But that shock was nothing compared
to the one she felt as her eyes turned slowly in stunned
realization to Drake. His face was flatly expressionless, jaw
set, eyes inscrutable. A thought leaped into her mind, tar-
geting on a wisp of uneasiness that had niggled at the back
of her mind, but which she had been unable to nail down
until this moment. At the store, Drake had called her Reva
Jonathan. Not just *Mrs*. Jonathan, as he would have if he'd
picked up the name from Beth. He had already known her
first name. And now she knew he had not wandered into
the store by chance.

"Unfortunately, my representative went into the meeting
without being as fully prepared as he should have been."
Drake's voice was as tightly controlled as his expression.

"We hadn't anticipated any opposition."

"Well, from what I hear, you sure enough got opposition." The man guffawed and slapped Drake on the shoulder. "Maybe that's what you deserve for beating me out on that demolition contract down at Coos Bay." The man walked to the counter and threw a leg over a stool next to the other two men.

Drake looked at Reva, his handsome features crystallized into an expressionless mask. "I own Century Development Corporation," he stated flatly.

Century Development Corporation—the company that had recently purchased the building in which her store was located. The company that planned to tear down the building and build a shopping mall. The company she had battled at the crucial city-council meeting. And Drake McQuaid was Century Development Corporation.

"That fact was finally beginning to dawn on me," she said grimly.

"I was just trying to figure out how to tell you. Perhaps I should have told you earlier." He scowled as he added the grudging admission.

No wonder he'd been so reluctant to talk about himself, Reva thought furiously. No wonder she'd had the vague feeling he was sidestepping her questions! Because he *was* detouring them, deftly and deliberately, and just as purposefully leading her into all that foolish chatter about herself. Pretending to be so interested in her. Showering her with outrageous flattery about her "gorgeous shoulders," telling her what a "lovely woman" and "pleasant view" she was. Telling her earnestly how much he admired her. Treating her to an expensive dinner—and a kiss!

And she had fallen for all of it, swallowed it all, as starry eyed as if she were starved for flattery and attention.

"I didn't start out with the deliberate intent to deceive you," he began. "But you weren't what I expected." He twisted the coffee cup in the saucer, his hand tense.

"I'm sure I wasn't! You must have jumped for joy when you realized what an easy mark I'd be for your experienced charm."

"Reva, that isn't true..."

Why hadn't she listened to that inner uneasiness that questioned his adroit deflection of her questions?

She knew the humiliating answer to that. She had been so wrapped up in her foolish suspicions about his marital status that she hadn't had time for other, more important suspicions. If she hadn't been so dazzled by his dark good looks and bold, virile charm, she'd have suspected he had some connection with Century Development when he first walked into the store and acted so interested in her plans. How incredibly naive of her to believe that he was interested in *her*.

Foolish, stupid, egotistical, she raged at herself. She cringed at the thought that she had actually listened to all those outrageously exaggerated compliments—and returned his kiss with almost abandoned passion!

Why had he done it? The answer was painfully obvious, of course. He had rapidly figured out that the quickest and most efficient way to get around her objections to his shopping-mall project was to pretend a fascinated interest in her. He'd do anything to push his damned project through, including seducing the opposition out of the way!

"Nice try, Mr. McQuaid," Reva said, "but it isn't going to work." Her smile was deliberately malicious.

"What are you talking about now?"

"I was a little slow catching on—and I probably wouldn't have caught on without your friend's help—but it finally did get through to me what this evening of wining and dining was all about."

"I told you, I planned to tell you myself that it was my company."

She ignored him. "You had it all figured out, didn't you? Flatter the poor little shop girl in her store. Wine and dine her at some expensive restaurant. Dazzle her with another layer of insincere flattery. And then—ah, the coup de grâce! Give her a real thrill, sweep her off her feet with a kiss!"

"I kissed you because—"

"All of it calculated to put the poor little shop girl in such a state of dithering excitement over you that she'd forget all about her objections to tearing the building down around her. You probably figured that, given the no-expenses-spared, no-holds-barred treatment, she—I—would be out there helping tear down the bricks with my bare hands!"

"Reva, you're getting unnecessarily excited before you know all—"

"Oh, but you're forgetting something," she said furiously. "I'm a 'hysterical broad,' and we hysterical broads get very excited!" Reva was well aware that the waitress and men at the counter were watching and listening with openmouthed interest, but she didn't care. She tried to stand up, but the table, mounted on an unmovable pedestal, blocked her way. Frustrated, she dropped back to the padded bench.

A flush of angry color rose under Drake's tan. "Those were Wheeler's words, not mine."

"True," she agreed. "But I'm sure you had others, equally descriptive. *Gullible* broad? *Man-hungry* broad? Pushover? Easy score?"

The color suffused his face now. "Reva..." There was warning in the single word, but she recklessly ignored it.

"How far were you willing to carry your inducements? To a midnight romp in your bedroom? Maybe go all out and have a week-long affair, instead of a skimpy one-night stand? Well, no thanks, Mr. McQuaid. I'm leaving. And you won't find me breaking my fingernails tearing down any bricks for you!"

"You're not going anywhere," Drake told her, "until we get a few things straight."

He had her trapped in the booth, his solid body an angry barrier between her and escape. His dark eyes flashed glitters of ice, and his jaw clenched rigidly.

With a sudden, reckless slash of her arm, Reva swept coffee cups, saucers, and a cascade of hot coffee over the edge of the table.

Drake gave a yelp of surprised outrage and leaped to his feet. Coffee cups crashed to the floor as he stared down at the hot flood of coffee on his pants.

Reva used the moment to grab her freedom, pausing for only a split second to note with malicious satisfaction that the coffee had landed in the vicinity of a man's most vulnerable area. Then she fled.

# Chapter Three

REVA WAS LITTLE more than out the door before she was
horrified by what she had done. She thought momentarily
of rushing back and apologizing, but her fleeing feet acted
of their own frantic volition to get her away from the scene
of humiliation as fast as possible. If ever anyone had lived
up to the description "hysterical broad," she thought in an
agony of embarrassment, she had. The simple awfulness of
what she had done washed over her in a hot tide. Why, oh
why, hadn't she acted with cool dignity and cut Drake
McQuaid down to size with razor remarks and slashing wit
instead of flinging coffee cups like some vindictive shrew?

How could she have been so terribly, foolishly gullible?
She had lapped up Drake's insincere flattery like a hungry
fish after bait. She had reacted to his touch like the sex-
starved divorcée he had cold-bloodedly calculated her to be.
Some men plied a woman with an expensive evening hoping
for sex in exchange. Drake McQuaid had arrogantly plied
her with dazzling hints of sex, hoping for cooperation on
his building project in return. He had obviously sized her
up as so frustrated and desperate and unattractive that she'd
jump at the chance for romantic involvement with a handsome man oozing sexy charm.

And she hadn't been all that far from leaping into his little trap, she thought with fresh humiliation as she remembered the shooting flames of desire he had wakened in her. She, who had always felt sex was as extravagantly overrated as the hyped-up advertising for some new television show.

The only smart thing she'd done, she thought grimly, was drive her own car to the inn so she had a speedy escape exit available. Perhaps her subconscious had had some premonition of trouble.

She was glad the following day was Sunday, so she would have time to gather her composure before going back to the store on Monday. Brian called Monday evening. He was all excited because Bax had promised to take him up to San Francisco to see a Giants' baseball game. He wanted Reva to be sure to tell Mark that he was going to see the Giants play. Following the activities of the professional teams was one of the interests Brian and Mark shared.

On Tuesday, Reva threw herself into the first of her projects for improving the store, a simple rearranging of products to make the aisles and counters more inviting for browsing. She had let herself get carried away with that heady feeling of freedom, Reva told herself in severe tones, or she would never have fallen for Drake McQuaid's flashy charm. She also had to admit, with an uncomfortable twinge of guilt, that some of her feeling of freedom had come from Mark's absence as well as Brian's. No more of that! Time to settle down to business. She was not a "while the cat's away, the mouse will play" sort of person.

She briskly set Beth, who had some artistic talent, to making hand-printed placards for each cheese, describing flavor characteristics and uses for each variety instead of merely naming it. Mrs. Parker had always had a take-it-or-leave-it attitude toward the more exotic cheeses and stuck to cheddar or mild Monterey Jack for herself, but Reva sampled everything.

That afternoon, Reva saw Drake and a couple of other men outside the front window of the store. Drake and one of the men were dressed in business suits, the other man was in tan workman's clothing. All three appeared to be studying the structure of the building, poking, prying, and measuring, and the professional-looking man was jotting something in a notebook. The following day the two men were back without Drake. Reva heard them rummaging around the hallway leading to the empty rooms upstairs, and later Beth reported she'd seen them poking around in the electrical boxes. Mrs. Depew, who owned the antique store two doors away, said they'd shown a lot of interest in the plumbing that had flooded her floor last winter. She also said that, when she asked what they were doing, they told her they were making an "evaluation of the building," whatever that meant.

Reva had already figured out what Drake and the men were doing. Drake hadn't given up on his plan. He was preparing for another assault on the city council, and this time Century Development would be armed with a barrage of arguments to support their application for tearing down the old structure and building a new shopping mall. They would be able to pinpoint each and every crumbling brick and corroded pipe in the old structure. They would assemble everything from legal to economic arguments, and then Century Development would roll over Reva's puny little protests like a tank over a blade of grass.

Oh, Drake was so clever, Reva thought bitterly. Getting her to talk about herself had served two devious purposes. It had diverted her attention away from pursuing incriminating questions about him, and it had given him a nice arsenal of information to use against her. Thanks to her big mouth, he knew she had no real financial resources to fight him, knew she couldn't afford legal or technical assistance. He knew her business experience was limited—and probably that her experience along more intimate lines was rather limited also.

Again she found herself returning to hot thoughts of the depth of physical effect Drake had aroused in her. Was it possible to be starved for something you had never really possessed, something you weren't even sure existed? It wasn't that she had ever disliked sex. She had approached lovemaking eagerly in her marriage, at least in the first years. But afterwards she had usually felt a small, dismayed sense of, "Is that all there is?" Later, of course, she'd felt so much held-back resentment and anger that true *love*making was probably impossible, and she merely went through the motions.

No matter what kind of unlikely physical reaction Drake had aroused in her, however, he was not going to ram his plan through without a further battle from her, she decided resolutely. Even if she hadn't his resources and had little chance of winning, she would give the fight her best shot. The old building had known a lot of the town's history and deserved to be preserved.

Yet in some small, traitorous corner of her mind, Reva could see Drake's point of view and understand why he wanted to tear down the old building and erect something new and modern. Over the years, tenants had gradually deserted until only Cheese 'n' Stuff, the antiques store, and the shoe store on the corner remained. And the shoe store was even now in the midst of a going-out-of-business sale. Until recently, a partnership of accountants had occupied a few rooms on the second floor, but the third floor had been empty for as long as Reva could remember. The former owners hadn't put the necessary money into repairs and modernization, and Mrs. Parker had spent some of her own money on this small portion of the building. From a purely economic viewpoint, a shiny new shopping mall that would attract large, prosperous new businesses had all the advantages. But surely economics wasn't all that mattered where history was concerned.

On Friday afternoon, Jill Anderson stopped by the store for a few minutes. She and her husband owned Razor Bay's one really good dress shop and had just returned from the buying trip to California on which they had generously let Brian ride along to visit his father. Jill was full of bright chatter about the trip and the new line of dresses they would soon be carrying.

"I ordered one cinnamon-pink silk that would be perfect

for you," Jill told her breezily. "It's backless, and the neckline plunges down to here." She indicated an area in the vicinity of Reva's navel.

Reva laughed. "Great. I can wear it when Mark and I take the kids camping."

Jill grimaced. "Knowing Mark, if he ever saw you in such a dress he'd rush around trying to make you decent with a coat or blanket."

Mark was not Jill's favorite person. She and Wally enjoyed their two children and did many things with them, but Jill always said firmly that she didn't believe parents should make their lives an endless carousel revolving around their children, the way Mark did around his daughter.

A brown United Parcel van pulled up outside just then, and the driver carried in a flat package. Reva signed for it while Jill looked on curiously.

"What's this?" Jill cried in mock consternation when she noted the name on the box, the discreet signature indicating that it was from one of Portland's more expensive emporiums. "My stuff too cheap for you these days?"

"Don't be ridiculous," Reva protested. "I didn't order anything."

She opened the box almost reluctantly, a suspicion forming in her mind. The suspicion was correct. She pulled back the tissue paper and unfolded a creamy white cashmere shawl so light and airy that it seemed to float in her fingers. It was far more expensive than the wrap she had lost. Jill fingered the metallic silver threads shot through the fabric. Them she pounced on a bottle of perfume in an exquisite crystal flacon.

"You've been holding out on me," Jill accused. "This is from a *man*. Not Mark. Who?"

There was no card, but Reva had no doubt about who had sent the package. "It's a long story," she said, hedging, not wanting to explain everything, even to this close friend whose encouragement had been instrumental in helping her make the decision to take the risks inherent in buying the store. "And it doesn't mean anything," she hastened to add.

Jill just smiled knowingly as she headed for the door.

"Okay. Keep your little secrets. But you can't keep hidden for very long the kind of man who sends stuff like *this*."

Reva folded the lovely spindrift of fabric and put it back in the box. Her feelings were mixed. She was flattered, of course. But the part of her that responded to the flattery was the same foolish part that had rushed recklessly to accept Drake's invitation, she reminded herself warningly, the same gullible part of her that drank in his compliments and responded as if they were some intoxicating wine.

But her feet were on solid ground now, and she knew what the expensive gift was. She had told Jill the gift didn't mean anything, but that wasn't true. What it meant was that Drake McQuaid was still trying to buy her cooperation. She might be only a minor stumbling block in his plans, but he intended to sweep through her resistance.

Reva debated with herself about returning the luxurious wrap, but she was undecided how to do it. Send it along with her next rent check? That would no doubt create a bit of a stir at the offices of Century Development!

However, that wasn't necessary. Drake McQuaid would undoubtedly be around to see what sort of impact his bribe had on her. She would wait for his appearance.

She halfway expected him to stride arrogantly into the store on Saturday, but he didn't. She told herself that she was relieved, not disappointed.

She spent Saturday evening washing her hair and doing some bookwork from the store. Mark called to say that he and Jade would be home sometime the following week. Reva relayed Brian's message about seeing a Giants' game. Brian called only moments after Reva finished talking to Mark. He was bursting with excitement. Tomorrow was the day his dad was taking him to the game.

Reva was pleased. Sometimes she had felt guilty for not providing Brian with a father before this, but now it appeared Bax was fulfilling the role as he should. Perhaps she needn't feel she was somehow letting Brian down by not marrying Mark yet.

Sunday morning was misty and damp, but by midafternoon the sun had burned the fog away and the breezy day was perfect for hiking along the beach. Reva decided to drive down to one of the more secluded areas where the driftwood was often especially beautiful.

She was packing a couple of sandwiches and an orange when the doorbell rang. She opened the door and stared at the dark-haired man standing there.

"How did you know where I live?" she asked, gasping. It was a ridiculous question, she realized the moment the words were out. It didn't take a supersleuth to find someone in Razor Bay. But the unexpected sight of Drake had stunned her. A rakish breeze lifted his dark hair and tossed it into crisp disarray. In open sunlight, his dark eyes had a warm, golden-brown gleam. He was wearing jeans and a silky, pearl-gray sportshirt with the top buttons open. He looked windswept and carefree, with a rough-edged sophistication and that same hint of danger in his dashing virility. In another life he might have been a pirate as easily as an aristocrat, Reva thought a little breathlessly.

"There's only one R. Jonathan in the Razor Bay phone book," he pointed out.

She abruptly reined her thoughts into control. "What do you want?"

"We didn't get to finish our conversation the other night due to an—ah—unfortunate accident."

Against her will her gaze slid uneasily to the affected portion of his anatomy below the belt. The form-fitting jeans outlined powerful contours and clung to a lean pelvis and flat abdomen above long-muscled thighs. The slip of her gaze did not escape him.

"Fortunately my love life wasn't permanently endangered," he commented wryly. "No thanks to you."

"I'm sure gasps of female relief went up all over the West Coast," Reva muttered.

"But probably not at 451 Manzanita Street right here in Razor Bay," he shot back.

A hot stain suffused Reva's face, but she refused to acknowledge it. "If you stopped by to see if the shawl you sent to replace my lost one arrived, it did," she said stiffly.

"I presume the shawl fits? They didn't appear to come in sizes."

"You picked it out yourself?" Reva asked, surprised. Somehow she had assumed he'd grabbed the phone and carelessly ordered something suitably expensive to impress—and bribe—her.

"I had to go back to Portland for a few days."

She had planned to return the gifts along with some biting remark, but she suddenly changed her mind. Just now returning the gifts seemed an act of rather childish petulance. It would be better to salvage whatever small amount of dignity remained after that humiliating performance at the inn.

"Both the shawl and perfume are very—lovely," she said, making use of that salvaged dignity as best she could. "Thank you."

"Now, may I come inside so we can finish our discussion? Or shall we carry on a shouting match out here in front of your neighbors?" He waved and flashed a pleasant smile to Mrs. Dawson next door. Mrs. Dawson was watering her azaleas, but she was so interested in the man at Reva's door that the spray cascaded unnoticed at a window.

"I was just leaving to take a walk on the beach."

"Fine. We'll walk together." His voice was also pleasant. "I have something to tell you."

Reva hesitated again. She was reluctant to let him accompany her, partly out of sheer stubbornness, and partly because she sensed within herself a dangerous vulnerability to his simmering virility. Even now there was a quivery little flutter in the pit of her stomach as he gave her a smile that carried both challenge and invitation.

"Very well," she said. "I'll get my jacket."

Without inviting him inside, she went to the hall closet, yanked out a hooded windbreaker, and then grabbed her lunch sack from the kitchen counter. On second thought, she went back to the refrigerator and tossed another orange into the sack. By the time Reva went back outside, Drake had walked over to the fence and was complimenting Mrs. Dawson on her showy azaleas.

"You're very good at that, aren't you?" Reva said with sarcasm when he returned.

"Good at what?"

"Lavishing compliments on unsuspecting females."

"I believe in giving credit where credit is due. I never give compliments I don't mean." His eyes roved boldly over her snug jeans and the clinging curve of her T-shirt. His eyes suddenly danced with wickedness. "Would you care to hear one now?"

Reva ignored the question and headed for her car parked in the driveway.

"We could go in my car," he offered.

"No," she insisted.

"Somehow I knew that's what you'd say."

For the first time she noted the pale yellow car almost hidden by the hedge around her yard. It was a modest compact, not what she would have expected from someone with Drake's flair and style.

"It's a rental car," he explained. "I left the Rolls at home in case one of my harem wanted the chauffeur to drive her somewhere."

He spoke in such an offhand, conversational tone of voice that Reva passed over the casual statement, then did a double take as the words sank in. When she realized he was making fun of her, she glared at him. Weird sense of humor.

"That is the rather ridiculous view you have of me, isn't it?" he chided gently.

"I'm sure I don't care how large a harem of women you have," she retorted. She was not about to have her attention diverted by more foolish curiosity about his marital status.

"But it is how you see me, isn't it?" he persisted.

"Perhaps." She opened the door of her car and tossed the hooded jacket and lunch sack in the back seat.

"I can assure you it is a long way from the truth. I don't have a Rolls, and my roll call of wives is limited to the one ex I already mentioned. I'm afraid you're under the mistaken impression that I can afford to buy a piece of property and just shrug my shoulders and take the loss if someone doesn't happen to like my plans for it."

What is this? Reva thought scornfully. Had he decided to switch tactics and play on her sympathies now? "You seem to live reasonably well," she said with some irony.

"You don't appear to be poised on the edge of poverty."

He nodded in agreement. "But I go into debt on every project I undertake, the same as practically every other businessman does. And in today's shaky economic climate, property development is not exactly a rock-solid proposition."

"Is this what you came to tell me?" she demanded.

A muscle twitched angrily along his angular jawline. "No."

Reva slid into the driver's seat. "Do you want to follow me in your car?" Reluctantly she added curiously, "Just why are you using a rental car?" Perhaps she had misjudged him, and the opposition she had aroused to his project really was a devastating financial blow.

He hesitated. "I use the company plane when I'm traveling around the state. It's out at the county airport."

"The problems of being an impoverished businessman," Reva murmured mockingly, taking back her moment of concern. She started the engine.

He went to the small car and got a denim jacket. He threw it into the back seat on top of her windbreaker and slid into the passenger's seat. "You see? I'm not taking my car. That proves I'm much more trusting and much less suspicious than you are." He flashed her a winning smile.

"Perhaps it only proves I'm not as dangerous a threat as you are," she retorted. She backed the car out of the driveway and headed south out of town.

"There you go again, using that word *dangerous* in connection with me, as if I shouldn't be allowed around virtuous women and small children," he chided. "You're going to give me a complex of some sort."

"I'm sure your male ego is strong enough to stand the strain."

"I'm not sure about that. You put quite a crimp in it the other night with your tigerish little display of temper," he said. He cast her a sideways glance. "Remind me never to corner you in a coffee-shop booth again."

Reva felt another sunburn-tinted flush steal over her face, but she determinedly kept her attention on her driving. The road skirted the beach for a couple of miles, then left it as the shoreline made a sweeping curve to the west. Reva passed up the stretch of easily accessible beach along the highway. The driftwood was always picked over there. She turned onto a gravel road and then left that to bounce along two sandy tracks through a coarse, head-high stand of tannish-green beach grass.

She parked the car in a widened turnaround area just under the high brow of sand edging the sloping beach. The waves could not be seen from this point, but the endless muffled roar declared their existence. Here, protected from wind by the barrier of heaped sand, the sunshine felt pleasantly hot. Reva retrieved her jacket from the back seat and threw Drake's denim jacket to him. In spite of the warmth here, the open beach was apt to be breezy enough to require the protective layer of clothing. She stuffed the sandwiches in one pocket, an orange in the other, and tossed the second orange to Drake.

"What's this?"

"Lunch."

"The way to a man's heart is through his stomach?" he suggested.

"If I were aiming at a man's heart, I'd use stronger ammunition than one deviled-egg sandwich and an old orange," Reva retorted.

"Ah, but that's all the ammunition some women need." Drake smiled wickedly and deliberately let his eyes run the length of her body. "Along with a few other—ummm—attractions."

Reva started up the steep hump of sand, angrily feeling he somehow always got the best of her in their verbal exchanges. She scrambled up the steep slope, slipping and sliding backward at least one step for every two she took upward, but she was careful not to grab at the cutting blades of rough grass. She was almost to the top when both feet slid out from under her in the soft sand. Drake was climbing right behind her, and her sliding feet smashed into his shins. He crashed down on top of her. And then they were both slipping and sliding and rolling down the steep incline, coming to rest in a hollowed pocket sheltered by the waving grass.

She was imprisoned beneath him, her body trapped intimately between his solid length and the warm sand. He brushed a tousle of chestnut hair out of her eyes, and a small rain of sand showered her face.

"Isn't this interesting," he said conversationally. "We go tumbling down the hillside together and when we stop we're like this, two halves of a whole fitting perfectly together. Perhaps fate is trying to tell us something." He made a small, intimate movement that emphasized the hand-in-glove fit of their molded bodies.

"What do you want?" Reva demanded angrily. He was making no move to roll away from her, making no effort at all to alter the intimate contact of their entwined bodies. If anything, he pressed closer. She could feel the beginnings of his unmistakable male arousal, and furiously she realized her body was responding with its feminine equal. Her T-shirt was pushed up over her breasts, and the warmth of his chest seeped through her bra, making her breasts strain against the barrier of lacy cups.

His lips touched the end of her nose. "You really want to know what I want right now?" There was laughter in his voice, but the words were only half teasing, and something beyond laughter smoldered in the dark depths of his eyes. To Reva, it was all too obvious what he wanted.

"Just let me up." She got her arms back and shoved at his shoulders. "I came here to walk on the beach, not wrestle in the sand!" The shove was ineffectual, but when she tried to twist away from him the only result was a suggestive friction between their bodies that heightened the pounding of her blood.

"There's a price to pay," he warned when she gave up the struggle and simply glared at him. "There's always a price to pay for freedom."

"What price?" she asked suspiciously.

His mouth dipped to hers, playfully at first, as if he were just teasing her for a moment by forcing her to acknowledge his greater strength before he let her up. But the teasing kiss was like the stray spark that unintentionally lands on dry tinder, and Reva's parted lips were the incendiary tinder that ignited under the spark. She tried to hold herself rigidly unresponsive, tried to douse the flame with scornful, drenching thoughts, but mere thoughts were no match for the flame of desire that made her return the sudden harsh clamp of his mouth with a fierce hunger.

Sunlight beat against her closed eyelids, and she felt as if a tiny light were growing larger and larger within her until it threatened to consume her in its incandescence. When he lifted his lips from hers, she realized her body was arched against his, straining for a contact that the barriers of clothing would not permit. Vaguely she became conscious of voices and the slam of a door. Another car had arrived.

And here she was, she thought, suddenly aghast at the incriminating situation, rolling in the sand with Drake like some oversexed adolescent.

"There's someone here," she whispered frantically.

His tongue teased the corner of her mouth and darted between her lips. "If we don't move, maybe they'll go away."

And then what? Reva wondered apprehensively. Her body seemed to go off on this wild, willful tangent of its own, responding to Drake's elemental maleness and ignoring her own mental fury with the man. But she was reasonably confident that they were hidden by the sand and waving clumps of grass, and she certainly did not care to suddenly pop into view among some group of strangers with her hair sandy and clothes disheveled. Worse, yet, they might *not* be strangers.

For the moment she acknowledged that she and Drake were trapped here together like clandestine lovers. He settled more comfortably against her, as if he were perfectly agreeable to a long siege.

"Comfortable?" he inquired.

"As comfortable as can be expected under the circumstances, I suppose," she answered, with as much aloofness as was possible under the enforced contact.

"I can't think of a more delightful place to make love

than right here in the sand and sunshine," he murmured.

For a moment Reva's mind played with the tantalizing thought. She never had...Then she came to her senses. "We're not making love!" she said fiercely.

He lifted his head to look down at her. "Lovemaking has many facets. It isn't always necessary to—"

"I am not interested in hearing your views on making love," she retorted in an acid whisper. "Just get to the point. You said you had something to tell me. What is it?"

"Must we always talk business?"

"I think it's about time we did talk business instead of getting sidetracked into other areas."

"Very well. He sighed regretfully. "As you may have noticed, I had an architect and my construction superintendent going over the building this past week. I don't have the architect's written evaluation yet, but in his preliminary report over the phone he said the building's plumbing and electrical systems are hopelessly outdated, but the building itself is structurally sound. Solid as a small mountain, in fact."

"And?"

"We've decided that, rather than raze the old building, we're going to restore and modernize it."

Reva's eyes widened and her lips parted in astonishment. "Really? Why, that—that's marvelous!"

"The plans are very much in the tentative stage at this point, of course, but we'll probably punch an open walkway through the center of the building and have small shops and boutiques opening off it. For the east end of the building, we'll try to attract some fairly large business, perhaps a furniture store, that will utilize all three floors. The rooms above the smaller shops will then be made into modern offices."

"Drake, that sounds terrific!" Reva responded enthusiastically. "I'm so surprised—and delighted! What brought this about?"

"Oh, various things. The architect's report on the structural soundness of the building; my own realization after going over tapes of the city council meeting that the building does have some important historical significance. The townspeople appear to be in favor of preserving the building, so there could be an extended battle and bad publicity over tearing it down. There are also some tax advantages to restoring a historical structure." His businesslike listing softened to a teasing smile. "One determined young lady's fiery resistance to tearing down the building was pretty persuasive, too."

"I honestly do believe the old building should be preserved. Even if my store weren't in it, I'd believe that." Without thinking, her fingertips traced the heavy, dark line of his eyebrows and explored the tiny character lines at the corners of his eyes. His hair fell across his forehead in boyish disarray. With this announcement she suddenly felt differently toward him, less stubbornly defensive. He was no longer the hostile adversary toward whom she felt a bewildering conflict of anger and attraction. Now the feeling was solely one of attraction . . .

"I doubt that this new plan will be nearly as profitable as the original one," he went on, "but dollars aren't the only consideration. I realize there are other important values in this particular situation."

"I—I'm sorry about the other night at the inn," Reva said. "What I did was really unforgivable."

"But effective." His voice held warm, husky laughter.

At some point he had slid to one side so his body no longer held her by brute force. She was also aware that the only sounds around them now were the background roar of the ocean and an occasional shriek of a gull. The other car had gone. Nothing held her now, but she felt no urge to leap to her feet and escape. In the engulfing warmth of sun and sand, with Drake lying next to her, she felt pleasantly languid. She dug a hip into the sand, edging a fraction of an inch closer to him, and he threw a companionable leg over her.

"I want to get something else straight," he said suddenly. "About last weekend."

"I'd rather just forget last weekend," Reva murmured ruefully.

"No. I don't like your suspicion that I asked you out just to circumvent your objections to my company's plans. To tell the truth, meeting you turned *everything* upside down."

"In what way?" Another button of his shirt had come undone and she combed her fingers through the dark mat on his chest, watching with interest the way the silky hair curled in dark rings around her fingers.

He caught her hand, halting its widening exploration. "Don't do that," he commanded.

"Why not?"

"Because it makes me forget what I'm talking about, and I want to tell you this."

"All right." Her voice was innocent but her lips twitched. "Tell me."

He went on to explain that, after receiving his representative's report about the city council's rejection of the company's plan, he had flown over to Razor Bay to assess the situation. He had gone to the cheese store expecting to find the proprietor about the same age as the building and approximately as attractive as its corroded plumbing. "Instead, there you were, looking like a pixie angel. And I found that instead of wanting to battle and argue with you, I wanted to kiss your bare shoulders."

Reva listened with lazy attention to his admission. She had promised not to comb her fingertips through his chest hair, but she hadn't promised not to run her palms under his shirt and across the long muscles of his back. The feel of smooth, pliant skin over hard muscle was strangely tantalizing.

"I was afraid to tell you right off who I was, of course. I figured you'd throw me out on my ear. But I thought that if we got to know each other, perhaps you could accept *me*, even if you couldn't accept my plan for the building." He gave her shoulder a small shake, demanding her full attention. "Okay? And I meant everything I said. I wasn't just giving you a lot of insincere flattery," he added almost fiercely.

"But you were thinking about seducing me."

"Not for any company benefit," he said in a husky voice.

"Strictly for my own. And I'm still thinking about it. If you keep running your hands over me like that—" He left the warning unspoken but used the leg thrown over her to wedge her pelvis against his solid frame. He cupped her breast with a warm hand.

Reva laughed breathlessly, suddenly aware of the dangers of her audacious behavior. What had gotten into her? She'd never felt any particular desire to explore Mark's anatomy, and now she couldn't seem to keep her hands off Drake. "I think it's time we took our walk," she said hurriedly.

"*I* think it's time we took a shower."

The *we* gave Reva instantaneous visions of the two of them naked and laughing under a cascade of shimmering water. From the gleam in Drake's eyes, she suspected his thoughts were keeping pace with hers—and probably outdistancing even her active imagination.

"We haven't even eaten our lunch," Reva protested.

He withdrew his leg, and she sat up and fished the sandwiches out of her pocket. They were mangled beyond identification, an unappetizing, squishy mess of bread, mayonnaise, and deviled egg.

Reva wrinkled her nose in distaste. "Ugh." She looked at him tentatively. "We could go back to my place and cook something."

Actually, it was several hours past lunchtime. The sun had dipped below the hillocks of sand.

He grinned. "Exactly what I had in mind." He leaned over her. "Put your arms around my neck," he commanded.

Alarmed, she drew back into the hollow of sand, but he repeated the command and she complied a little hesitantly. With her arms around his neck, he pulled them both to a standing position at the same time. He kissed her on the nose.

"See? I make a perfectly innocent suggestion and you immediately have all sorts of dark suspicions." But his punishment for her suspicion was merely another kiss, sweet with promise.

Back at the house, Drake accepted Reva's offer of a

shower to wash off the sand, though he looked disappointed when she sidestepped his hint about her joining him. She washed up and brushed the sand out of her hair, then whipped up a quick supper of cheese omelet and crab salad.

Drake emerged from the shower with gleaming damp hair and a fresh, soapy male scent. The meal was companionable. He did not avoid Reva's questions this time, and she learned he was thirty-three years old and an engineering graduate of a small West Coast university. His parents were divorced and each remarried to a new partner. His own marriage, to a girl he met at college, had taken place shortly after graduation. He then went to work for her father's construction and development firm in Portland.

Drake smiled wryly when he saw Reva's eyebrows lift slightly in response to that bit of information. "You're thinking I married her to get ahead, because she was the boss's daughter?"

"The thought occurred to me."

He lifted his shoulders in a small shrug. "Who knows? Maybe I did, since it turned out we hadn't much in common. But if I did marry her to get into her father's company, I very shortly had a rude awakening. The company was on the edge of bankruptcy. Gale's father had started the company on inherited money and mismanaged it every step of the way. He finally decided to sell out before the company went under. I managed to borrow enough to take over the company. Gale didn't think I could make it. She deserted like the proverbial rat from a sinking ship."

"Are you sorry the marriage didn't last?"

"I don't like admitting failure, even the failure of a lousy marriage," he acknowledged. "But no, I'm not sorry now, and I'm glad there weren't children to complicate the situation." He suddenly reached across the table and cupped Reva's chin in his hand. "And this is the only discussion I ever intend to have with you about that past marriage. It's over and done with, and whatever feelings were once there are long dead. Okay?"

He looked deeply into her eyes and she nodded in agreement. Then they went on to have coffee and dessert. Drake laughed when he saw the dessert was homemade cheese-cake, saying he should have guessed, but he enthusiastically downed two big wedges of the creamy concoction. "That's much stronger ammunition than one egg sandwich and an old orange," he teased meaningfully. Then they shared more coffee and talk and laughter.

There had been no discussion between them about spending the night together, but Reva knew the evening was headed that way. The intent lay in Drake's smoldering glance, even as he talked lightly of other things. Perhaps she should make some protest now, Reva thought uneasily; explain that she was enormously attracted to him, but she wasn't quite ready to—

Oh, but she was ready, some inner voice argued recklessly. Her body was alive with memories of his touch, eager for more, breathless in anticipation of the possibility of something above and beyond what she had ever before known in the realm of making love. An excitement simmered in the air between them, heightening each word and look.

Yet some old-fashioned restraint made her revive the conversation that had suddenly lagged as Drake looked at her with an intensity of meaning in the glowing depths of his dark eyes.

"How soon will you start work on the building?" she asked brightly. She jumped up and reached for the coffee maker to refill their cups.

He smiled as if he well knew what she was doing, but he answered just as if the atmosphere weren't thick with the sensual awareness between them. "As soon as possible. In fact, the workmen will probably start tearing out some of those strange, tiny rooms immediately."

Reva laughed. "I think the third floor was once used as a jail."

"The shoe store closed up shop yesterday, of course, and they'll be out by midweek. Mrs. Depew's lease on the antique store is up at the end of the month. So that leaves only—"

Reva's hand stopped, the coffee maker poised over his

cup as a dark suspicion suddenly leaped into her mind. He couldn't be saying . . . But he was.

"I'm sure you've already realized the building will have to be empty during the reconstruction." His expression was guileless as he looked up at her. "All tenants will have to be out by the end of the month."

# Chapter Four

REVA STARED AT him in shocked disbelief. She set the coffeemaker down without refilling the cups. "You can't be serious! I can't possibly move the business somewhere else. Surely it isn't really necessary—"

"Reva, this isn't some minor remodeling project." Drake sounded mildly impatient, as if she were being unnecessarily dense. "The architect, the construction superintendent, and the company's legal counsel are all agreed that the building should be empty during renovation."

"You can overrule them! It's *your* company," Reva cried. "I just can't—" She shook her head, on the verge of sudden tears. She felt a panicky helplessness, as if she were standing at the bottom of some insurmountable peak. She hadn't the financial resources to relocate the store elsewhere. She was already deeply in debt. Even if she could raise money for a move, a few weeks without business—and income— would be financially disastrous. And even if she were willing to make a move, there was no place to go. Haltingly she tried to explain all this to Drake.

"Reva, I'm not unsympathetic to your problems, but the construction crews will be tearing into walls and floors and ceilings to redo the electricity and plumbing and install a modern heating system. Cutting the walkway will require structural reinforcement. There will be dangerous equipment working, and the whole area will be dusty and noisy." Drake's voice balanced on the fine edge of exasperation now, as if he were drawing on every ounce of self-control to maintain his patience with her.

His explanation barely penetrated Reva's numbed shock. A fresh suspicion suddenly tumbled into her mind. "You just want me out! Perhaps you don't even intend to renovate the building. Once you get everyone out, maybe you'll just ram ahead with your original project!" She glared at him in accusation.

Drake leaned forward. His tanned hand gripped the empty coffee cup so tightly that the knuckles gleamed. "And what I'm hearing now is rather different from your impassioned plea to the city council to save a 'precious part of Razor Bay's historical heritage.'" He mimicked her words with cutting accuracy, his patience thinned to a knife edge. "But now when I work out a plan to save the building, it appears your motives aren't so noble and unselfish after all. Your only concern is for yourself. *Your* problems. *Your* inconvenience."

"That isn't true!" Reva said with a gasp, but her words faltered. She did believe the historical building should be preserved, but would she have fought to save it if her own financial security were not at stake?

"You want Century Development to make a big sacrifice to save the building, but you're not willing to—"

"You didn't plan to tell me this until morning, did you?" Reva asked, cutting angrily into his accusation with one of her own. "You planned to stay the night and then spring this on me in the morning!"

His expression went momentarily blank. "I don't know that I really thought about it." Wariness replaced the blankness. "I suppose I assumed it was obvious that the building would have to be empty while the work was in progress."

He'd done it again, Reva thought, wrath suddenly overtaking her panic. "Now I see the point of this afternoon's little drama," she said bitterly.

"Now what the hell are you talking about? What 'drama'?"

"Act One: You tell me how you've generously decided not to tear down the old building, being careful to make me feel I was an important factor in your decision, of course. Act Two: You spend the night with me. Make love to me. By morning I'm so dazzled by your virile expertise that Act Three is a foregone conclusion."

Drake leaped to his feet. His chair crashed to the floor, but he paid it no heed. Impending explosion menaced behind the tight control on his face. He grabbed Reva by the shoulders and shook her lightly. "You are the most stubborn, unreasonable—"

Reva ignored what she suspected was only the beginning of a long list of damning adjectives. "The foregone conclusion of Act Three, of course," she went on relentlessly, "is that I'm so grateful for your attention and in such a romantic dither that I meekly pick up my cheese and steal away into the night, thereby leaving the way clear for you to proceed with your plans."

"I doubt that you do anything *meekly,*" Drake cut in grimly.

"Talk about *women* using sex to get ahead in business!" she said, storming at him. "Act One worked nicely. Act Two was well on its way to success, but—"

"Reva, I did not have in mind making love to you because of that damned building!" he told her, raging. Anger turned his chiseled mouth into a thin, uncompromising line. His grip on her upper arms tightened, and for a moment she thought he was going to fling her across the room. Instead he kissed her, a savage assault that seared her mouth like rough whiskey. His mouth ground against hers, as if he must punish her with passion to keep himself from inflicting some even more violent physical damage on her.

A hot tide of response surged through her, no less powerful because it was unexpected and utterly unwanted. She felt streaks of lightning race through her veins, sparks of arousal explode within her. Somehow she channeled the explosive force into fury instead of passion. She twisted her head from side to side and finally wrenched her mouth away from his. "And if sweet seduction doesn't work," she said, panting, "try brute force!"

He growled an oath and thrust her away from him, not hard enough to fling her across the room but hard enough to shove her ungently into a chair.

"If you'll just control yourself..." he began. His rigid arm pinned her in the chair.

"And not act like a 'hysterical broad guarding her virginity,'" she finished for him. "Well, I am *not* calm. You're practically throwing my business out in the street."

She broke off as it finally dawned on her that she was panicking too soon. Drake had felt it necessary to turn the full force of his seductive charm on her for a reason. A very *good* reason. She had a potent weapon to use against him. He couldn't just toss her out on the street! And that weapon, of course, was the lease. She had that signed bit of paper, the agreement originally made between the woman from whom she had bought the store and the former owners of the building, but now fully binding on both Drake and Reva. And it had two years yet to run!

She had every right to be furious with his use of underhanded tactics to get her business out of his building, but there was no reason to rush headlong into panic. She tried to impose some order on the patchwork jumble of thoughts in her mind. She should have reminded him coolly at the beginning of this conversation that she had the lease and had no intention of letting him force her out of the building simply because her presence there was inconvenient for him. She was only demeaning herself by bringing in all these accusations about his personal behavior toward her.

She forced an aloof calm into her voice. "As we are both well aware, I have a perfectly legal lease on my portion of the building. And I do not intend to move my business elsewhere."

He released her shoulder and massaged his hand as if the harsh grip had cramped it. "I wasn't planning to throw you out in the street," he told her. "Century Development is fully prepared to buy out the lease. I'm sure we can come to some satisfactory financial agreement. I don't expect you to move to another location without—"

She stood up, hazel eyes shooting golden sparks. "Don't expect me to do it at all!" she told him furiously.

"Reva, you're being unreasonable," he warned tightly. "You're letting a personal anger with me affect your business decisions."

"Why should I be angry with you?" Her voice oozed silky sweetness. She felt more in control of herself now. In fact, she felt quite in control of the entire situation. "You afforded me a most pleasant afternoon snuggling in the sand. And you've given me a marvelous education in the methods some men use to conduct business with women."

"This is your final word then?" His voice was as stiff as his ramrod backbone. "You won't accept a reasonable offer from Century Development to buy out your lease?"

"No doubt you'd be willing to supply some—ummm—fringe benefits in addition to a monetary consideration?" She taunted recklessly. "Give your all for the company?"

A stain of color beneath his skin darkened his tan. He snatched his denim jacket from the floor where it had fallen with the chair and stalked to the door. "You'll be hearing from me again," he said ominously over his shoulder just before the door slammed violently enough to jar the neighborhood.

Reva felt a momentary apprehension. Only minutes before, the room had held the delicious warmth of intimacy, but now it had a shivery chill. She wrapped her arms around herself, suddenly cold. What would he do now? Nothing, she assured herself. He was just making impotent threats because his arrogant, macho plan of seduction hadn't worked.

Yet *impotent* was not a word that fit Drake McQuaid . . .

Reva showered and washed the final grits of sand out of her hair. She slipped into a peach-colored shortie nightgown and slid into bed, but reruns of the day's events played endlessly through her mind. Oh, the things she should have done, the things she should have said!

Why had he tried again today what was really just a variation of the ploy he had tried on her at the inn? No doubt because he had such an inflated view of his irresistible attraction to women that it was inconceivable to him that one woman could resist him twice.

And she hadn't been resisting him, she thought with renewed disgust with herself. She had been ready to spend the night with him, eager to make love with him! If that one small, vital bit of information about having to move her business hadn't slipped out prematurely, he'd probably be here in her bed right now.

Her mind lingered momentarily on that thought, rolling it around like some forbidden, sinfully delicious tidbit. She could almost feel his presence in the room—husky laughter . . . sweetly tantalizing kisses and caresses deepening into hungry demand . . . lovemaking that rose to undreamed of heights of passion . . .

She forced her thoughts ahead to picture the next morning. No doubt, over bacon and eggs, he'd have mentioned with offhand carelessness something like, "Oh, by the way, you'll have to move your store out of the building by the end of the month." How would she have reacted at that point?

With fury, of course, she assured herself. Drake might have wound up with not only hot coffee in his lap, but a platter of bacon and eggs as well.

Yet she wasn't really sure that that was what would have happened. She had a strange, tremulous feeling about making love with Drake, as if with him she might leap into a wild new world of soaring passion from which there was no turning back. Perhaps his scheme would have worked. Perhaps one night of love would have made her his willing slave.

Oh, this is ridiculous, she thought, chastizing herself scornfully. His ulterior motives *had* slipped out, and he *wasn't* here in her bed, and she most certainly was not his slave. All this speculation was mere foolishness. She got up, took two aspirins with half a glass of milk, and finally fell asleep.

On Monday the shoe-store people started dismantling their almost-empty racks. Mrs. Depew received a brief but courteous note from Century Development saying her lease would not be renewed at the end of the month. Mrs. Depew was not overly upset. Her "gentleman friend" ran a second-hand store out on the highway, and she could share a portion of his building. Reva suspected Mrs. Depew had her eye on the possibility of a marriage merger as well.

Reva neither heard nor saw anything of Drake that day, and her uneasiness increased. The silence felt ominous. Then one of her refrigerated display counters suddenly stopped working. She called a repairman, who found the problem to be with the building's wiring rather than with her refrigerated unit. He repaired the wire but warned that it was only a stopgap solution.

Coincidence? Of course, Reva assured herself. Drake had too much pride and male ego to resort to something as underhanded as tampering with the electricity. Yet who knew what lay behind the dark enigma of his handsomely chiseled features?

Mark called Tuesday afternoon. He'd just gotten back from Seattle. He said Jade's grandparents had sent along a box of lovely Washington apples, and he'd bring some over that evening. Reva hesitated a moment and then, puzzled and a little annoyed with herself for the hesitation, she invited Mark and Jade to dinner.

Reva had a pastry-crusted meatloaf and scalloped potatoes baking in the oven by the time Mark and Jade arrived that evening. Ten-year-old Jade presented Reva with a sack of apples, exchanged hugs with her, and then dashed to the stove. She opened the oven door and sniffed deeply of the escaping aroma.

"I *love* your meatloaf," she announced.

Reva laughed. Who but a ten-year-old girl could be so dramatic about meatloaf? Jade was never shy about voicing her preference for Reva's cooking over her father's uninspired meals.

"That's why I made meatloaf for you, sweetie," Reva said, smiling. "Welcome home."

Mark kissed her on the cheek. "Hi, hon. You're looking terrific." He held up a big package. "Present."

The present was a new popcorn popper, one of the newer

hot-air types. Reva was pleased, of course. The kids always enjoyed popcorn, and her old popper was erratic at best. It was a practical, useful gift. But just for a moment Reva felt as if the present were more for the children than for her, that it somehow put her in the class of a useful household appliance, too. Then she was ashamed of the ungrateful thought. She put it aside, hugged Mark, and said they'd try out the popcorn popper later in the evening.

Jade chattered animatedly through dinner, all about eating in the revolving restaurant atop the Space Needle in Seattle and riding the speeding monorail. Afterwards they gathered around the phone and Reva dialed Bax's number in San Jose. She had waited until now to call Brian, knowing he'd want to tell Mark all about seeing the San Francisco Giants play. He and Mark shared a superior-male conspiracy about baseball that excluded Reva.

Mikki answered the ring, then called Brian to the phone. They talked a few minutes. Reva thought Brian sounded rather dispirited.

"Is anything wrong, hon?" she finally asked anxiously.

"No."

"Mark is here. He'd like to hear all about your trip to the ball game."

There was a slight hesitation before Brian said with a small-boy attempt at indifference, "We didn't go."

"You didn't? Why not?"

"I dunno. I guess it was too far or something."

No farther than it had been when Bax promised to take him, Reva thought angrily. With a strained effort to censor the anger out of her voice, she told Brian that perhaps he and his father would be able to go to a game later on in the summer.

"Yeah," Brian agreed without coviction. "Maybe."

*Damn, damn, damn,* Reva murmured softly, helplessly, to herself. Brian's disappointment and hurt made her ache for him, but there was nothing she could do.

Mark took the phone then, his voice firm and cheerful. He told Brian he'd heard soccer teams for elementary-school children were going to form this fall, and evidently Brian was interested in that. By the time Reva took the phone again to tell Brian good-bye, he sounded more like his usual self. Reva gave Mark's hand a grateful squeeze.

They made popcorn. Jade took hers into the living room to munch in front of the television set. Mark and Reva sat in the kitchen with cups of coffee. The fluffy, hot popcorn was delicious, but Reva took only an occasional nibble. She couldn't get her mind off Brian's disappointment. How could Bax have done that to him, build up his hopes and then disappoint him! She listened with only a shallow portion of her attention while Mark talked about the Seattle school system.

She didn't even realize he had stopped talking until the silence stretched to an awkward length.

"I hear you had dinner at the inn while I was gone," Mark finally said in a casual tone of voice. "With a tall, dark, mysterious, and very handsome stranger." He kept the comment light, as if he weren't taking the description too seriously.

"Were you talking to Ann Hamilton?" Reva asked.

Mark nodded.

Reva shrugged. "It was just business. He's my landlord, actually. The owner of Century Development. Drake McQuaid."

"Was Ann's description accurate?"

"More or less. The company has decided not to tear down the building. They're going to renovate it instead." She didn't feel it necessary to explain to Mark that this bit of information had come from a second meeting with Drake.

"That should be good news for you."

"Not exactly." Reva grimaced. "The company says the building must be vacant while they work on it. They offered to buy out my lease, but I turned down the offer."

Mark considered that thoughtfully, taking a measured sip of coffee before asking, "How much was the offer?"

"I don't know. I didn't ask. The discussion didn't get that far. I'm just not interested in moving the store to a different location. They can work around me."

Mark walked over to the kitchen counter, returned with

the coffee maker, and refilled the coffee cups. "Do you think it was wise to turn down the offer before you even knew what it was?" he questioned finally.

A reasonable point, Reva admitted, but the very reasonableness of the question and Mark's thoughtful attitude somehow scratched on her nerves. Carefully she explained all the reasons she couldn't possibly manage a move, even if the lease buy-out were fairly generous. Somehow she also resented having to explain all this to Mark. If he had any real interest in her business, he'd *know* the problems involved.

"And then today I had trouble with one of the refrigerated units," Reva added crossly. "Actually, it was something wrong with the wiring in the building, not my refrigerated unit, but it was still a big bother."

"Will the landlord pay for the repair?" Mark asked.

"I presume so. I certainly intend to submit the bill to Century Development."

"And if they don't pay?"

Reva looked at him, her mood still on the surly side. "I don't see what you're getting at. According to the lease, they pay for repairs such as that."

"Hon, I really think perhaps you acted too hastily in turning down—"

"Mark, the man is an arrogant, insufferable Don Juan who thinks he is irresistible to women!"

"But you managed to resist him?" Mark inquired. He sounded more teasing than worried or suspicious.

"Yes!"

Reva felt flustered and angry, though at the moment she wasn't quite certain with whom she was angry. Mark didn't even seem ruffled by the fact that she'd had dinner alone with Drake.

"I still think you should reconsider the company's offer to buy out the lease, even if it isn't overly generous. Don't you see how difficult they can make things for you?" Mark said. "They can delay or ignore payment on bills such as this one. They can hassle you about all sorts of minor details. If you persist in hanging on during renovation of the building, they can make conditions so intolerable you won't have any business. And what recourse will you have? All you can do is break the lease and move out. Which is exactly what they want you to do anyway."

Reva acknowledged unhappily the accuracy of Mark's well thought out argument. Drake McQuaid could make life so difficult for her that she would wish she had, in the sarcastic words she had flung at him, meekly picked up her cheese and crept off into the night.

"I really do think the best solution would be to aim for the most satisfactory settlement you can make with the company, and let it go at that," Mark advised.

"I suppose so," Reva agreed reluctantly. She hated the idea of caving in to Drake's demands, of letting him win without a scrap. "But I have no idea where I'd move the store."

"You could just give it up and marry me," Mark suggested with a small smile. When that brought no response from Reva, he added, "There's an empty building over on Slough Street. I think a shoe-repair shop used to be there."

Mark had so little understanding of her business problems, Reva thought, sighing inwardly, though she said nothing aloud. The location he mentioned was on a back street where people would practically need a guide to find it. Yet his assessment of the situation with Century Development was astute enough. They could hassle her to death. Better to do as he said and try to get as much money from the company as possible on the lease buy-out, and simply make the best of a bad situation. Tomorrow she'd call a real-estate office and see if they knew of any suitable vacancies.

"You might be able to get a pretty good settlement out of Century Development," Mark said musing. "The company must have been considerably rattled for the owner to come here to talk to you personally.

To say nothing of what else he was willing to do personally, Reva thought sourly. She nibbled absentmindedly at a buttery chunk of popcorn. "What did you think when Ann first told you she'd seen me at the inn with this 'handsome, mysterious stranger'?" Reva asked finally.

"I assumed you'd have a reasonable explanation, which you do, of course."

Mark's answer was also calm and reasonable, of course. He was seldom impulsive or excited, never reckless. His calm response was based on the assumption that they were both responsible, reasonable, and intelligent adults. Yet for a moment Reva felt a most *un*reasonable frustration with him, a wild wish that he would have reacted with a little more fire and a little less restraint. How would Drake McQuaid have reacted under similar circumstances? The thought that he would calmly accept a report that a woman he was seeing regularly had been out with another man was laughable. She could easily picture Drake roaring into Cheese 'n' Stuff, ready to tear her and/or the man apart with his bare hands.

Yet that picture was faulty also, she realized, feeling unexpectedly dispirited again. Drake McQuaid didn't care what she did, except in how it affected his damned building.

"I guess I'd better get Jade home," Mark said. "It's been a long day. How about hamburgers and a movie at the drive-in Friday night?"

Reva automatically accepted the invitation. The drive-in was one of their standard weekend activities, along with roller skating, events connected with the schools, or cards with the Hamiltons and some other friends of Mark's. Mark was no more fond of Jill and Wally Anderson than they were of him, so Reva didn't see as much of them as she would have liked. Reva suspected Mark considered Jill, with her strong involvement in running the dress store, a bad influence on Reva.

The following morning Reva made several phone calls. The first was to a real-estate agency, asking them to check on commercially zoned vacancies in the area. The next call was to Drake at the inn. She planned to tell him she'd decided to accept his offer to buy out the lease. *After* she bargained with him for an acceptable sum, of course. She was braced to talk to him, had her arguments lined up like cannonballs ready to fire, and then she was frustrated with the inn's report that Drake had checked out. She debated with herself about calling the company offices in Portland, but decided against that action just yet. Let him stew for a few days wondering what kinds of problems she was going to give him. A few more days would also give her time to make an accurate assessment of rental possibilities.

Jill Anderson dropped by the store that afternoon, on her way to the bank. She invited Reva over for dinner Friday night. A Japanese friend was passing through and had promised to fix sushi.

"Why don't you bring along the sender of that gorgeous cashmere shawl?" Jill suggested.

Reva laughed, knowing Jill was fishing for information. "I'd love to. I mean, I'd love to come to your dinner," she amended, to make clear she wouldn't love to invite the sender of the shawl. "But Mark and I already have plans to go to the drive-in." She momentarily considered trying to talk Mark into the Japanese dinner at the Anderson's, but she decided against it. Mark would come if she insisted, but he'd be uncomfortable the whole evening and make her uncomfortable too. Jade was adventurous as far as food was concerned, but Mark regarded anything unusual with suspicion.

"Very well, don't tell me who your mysterious benefactor is." Jill sniffed, pretending to be aggrieved.

"I'll tell you this much," Reva retorted. "He's no benefactor." ·

The truth of that statement was made harshly clear Friday morning when the postman delivered the mail. There was a certified letter, return receipt requested. Reva signed for it, then, leaving Beth to watch the store, carried the letter to the back room before tearing the envelope open.

As she read the letter, Reva sank stunned to the single bed that still occupied the back room, a relic of the elderly former owner's need to get off her swollen feet occasionally. She reread the letter twice, though the words were quite clear. They were as brilliantly sharp as the cutting edge of a diamond. The new sign she had erected violated the terms of her lease. Century Development was, on that basis, thereby declaring the lease null and void. The premises were to be vacated by the end of the month. The letter bore Drake McQuaid's slashing signature.

So this was the result of Drake's ominous threat that she would be hearing from him again. He'd had this next step in mind even as he plied her with kisses and caresses!

Could he really do this? Reva rushed to her old oak desk, snapped on the stained-glass lamp, and pawed frantically through papers until she came up with a copy of the lease. She had glanced at it when she bought the business, of course, but her inspection had been superficial, to say the least. Mrs. Parker had said the same lease, except for a raise in rates on renewal, had been in effect for years, and there had never been any problems.

Now, among a fine-print listing of things the lessee must not do, Reva discovered a prohibition against any signs projecting from the building.

This is ridiculous! Reva stormed, unconsciously pacing the small room like a caged animal. Most of the prohibitions on the list were archaic restrictions somehow carried over from lease to lease without regard to their current applicability. Spittoons must be maintained in a clean and sanitary condition! Lessee must not allow loitering of undesirable persons or offer merchandise of inferior quality for sale.

Surely Drake couldn't enforce this interfering nonsense! And even if he could, surely a landlord must by law allow some minimum amount of time for correction of a violation. Oh, but correction would mean tearing down her marvelous new sign! No, she would get a lawyer and fight this unreasonable—

Reva's furious thoughts slammed to an abrupt halt. Lawyers. Fight. Expenses. Delays.

This was just the first in the endless hassle Mark had predicted. They would harass her with one detail after another until she'd be only too glad to get out. One way or another, Century Development was going to win, and she might as well grit her teeth and swallow that sour fact right now. And she had naively thought that not hearing from her would make Drake "stew."

It was Reva who stewed for most of the day. She knew

she might as well call the company and get it over with, but she kept delaying, worrying the thought around in her head like picking at a painful hangnail—and with no more fruitful results.

Finally, sighing, she picked up the phone and dialed direct to Century Development's Portland office. She might be beaten, but she intended to hold out for the most she could get from the company for giving up the lease.

A middle-aged female voice informed Reva politely that Mr. McQuaid had already left the offices for the weekend. He could be reached at the Inn of the Shaman Mask on the coast. The woman efficiently furnished the number.

Reva's hand still clutched the phone after she replaced the receiver. What was Drake doing back in the Razor Bay area? Thinking up some fresh way to harass her? Obviously he was through with inducements. Now he was into threats.

She dialed the inn nervously and asked for Mr. McQuaid. There was no answer when the operator rang his room. Would she care to leave her name and have Mr. McQuaid return her call? Reva gave her name and had just started to give her phone number when the female voice interrupted.

"Oh, Miss Jonathan, Mr. McQuaid left a message here for you when you called. I have it here . . . Yes, you're to meet him for cocktails in the Sea Lion Room at seven o'clock.

Surprise and then outrage made Reva unable to do more than mutter a strangled thanks to the deliverer of this insolent invitation. No, not an invitation, she corrected herself in a boil of rage, a command. Drake McQuaid had arrogantly *commanded* that she appear before him at the appointed time and place. No doubt with head properly bowed in deference.

She would not do it, of course. She was not about to dance on Drake McQuaid's puppet strings! She would meet him—if she met him at all—on *her* terms. If he thought she'd present herself meekly at the Sea Lion Room at seven o'clock, he could just think again. Perhaps Drake McQuaid had never been stood up by a woman before, but he was certainly going to get a taste of the experience now.

Reva's defiant rage lasted until closing time. By then the

rage had not abated, but the defiance had been tempered by a certain wary apprehension. If she intended to bargain with Drake on the lease, she had to see or at least talk to him personally. If she refused to meet him tonight, he would be quite capable of evading her for as long as he desired— until time ran out.

Reluctantly she called Mark and told him that she was going to be late that night. Briefly she explained about the threatening eviction letter and that she had a short meeting scheduled with Mr. McQuaid.

His reaction was one of mild annoyance, not so much because she had an appointment with another man, she suspected, but because her business problems were carrying over into private hours. There was also a bit of "I told you so" in it. She said she'd come by his house as soon as her meeting with Drake was over.

Reva didn't eat anything before leaving for the inn. She planned to make this meeting with Drake short and businesslike and then hurry back to hamburgers and the movie with Mark and Jade.

She showered and then, in sheer, ice-blue panties and bra, stood in front of her closet, one bare foot tapping the floor indecisively. She did not intend to dress up as if she were presenting herself for some command performance for Mr. Drake McQuaid's pleasure. She would wear what she usually wore to the drive-in movie, jeans and a simple blouse.

Defiantly she went one step further and put on one of her oldest, most faded pairs of jeans and a T-shirt Brian had once picked out for her. It was a brilliant hot pink and adorned with a cartoon of a smug-looking cat. If she didn't come up to the inn's—or Drake's—dress standards, that was just too bad!

A bank of hazy fog hovered offshore, but the sky overhead was clear as Reva drove up the coast to the inn. She parked and dashed up the stone steps. Her mutinous bravado suffered a few cracks as she saw several well-dressed couples on their way to the dining room, and she was uncomfortably aware of her own disreputable attire. This time, however, she was not unprepared for Drake, and she immediately spotted him standing off to one side of the lounge entrance.

He was also less formally dressed than on their former meeting at the inn, but hardly as casually attired as Reva. He wore gray flannel slacks and a burgundy cashmere pullover over a white shirt. He looked relaxed yet dashing, and his flashing smile added that small hint of polished danger that always sent a small shiver through her.

She felt at a distinct disadvantage in her old clothes, like the poor little tenant girl coming begging to the superior lord of the manor. She was suddenly aware of the way the worn jeans hugged her derriere, and that the clingy T-shirt left little to the imagination... though there was a speculative glint in Drake's eyes that hinted he was imaginatively supplying what little the T-shirt kept concealed. Damn him! She should have armed herself with every advantage possible, swept into the inn groomed and dressed to the eyebrows, as if she were doing him a favor by appearing!

"You suggested cocktails in the Sea Lion Room?" Reva challenged, lifting her head arrogantly as if she wore diamonds instead of a cartoon cat on her chest.

"Indeed I did," he agreed smoothly.

# Chapter Five

DRAKE TOUCHED HER elbow and guided her through the cavelike entrance to the Sea Lion Room with as much deference as if she were attired in satin and sable. Inwardly she raged at him, suspectiong he was deliberately making fun of her, but what could she say? She could hardly tear into the man for treating her with this polished courtesy, even though they both knew it was a mockery.

"White wine?" he inquired when they were seated.

"Please." At least in the dimly lit lounge her disreputable jeans were not so obvious, though the ridiculous cat cartoon on her chest felt as if it were outlined in neon. She brushed a nervous hand across her hair.

He leaned back in his chair, waiting for her to speak first. She had the feeling he was enjoying her all too obvious discomfort.

"I tried to call you in Portland. A secretary said you were staying here for the weekend." The words came out accusing.

"This renovation project has top priority with the company right now. I presume you received the company's letter?"

"I received *your* letter," she retorted pointedly. She wasn't going to let him get away with hiding behind the "company" shield, blaming architects and construction superintendents for a decision he had made.

"It's purely a business matter, of course. No hard feelings, I hope."

"No more than if I'd been knocked down and trampled by a wild stallion."

"A wild stallion," he mused. Their drinks arrived and he swirled the ice cubes lightly in his glass. "I do believe this is the first time I've ever been called that."

"Perhaps the term 'stud' is more familiar. Though it is usually used in a somewhat different context, of course."

"I think I'm being—ummm—obliquely disparaged," he observed. Quite correctly. He did not, however, appear particularly perturbed.

"Perhaps you'd care to hear a few even more descriptive terms?" Reva suggested. She felt frustrated with her inability to get a rise out of him with her taunts. He looked more amused than annoyed. He could afford to be amused, she thought sourly. He was winning their small war. All she could do now was try to salvage something from the lease buy-out.

He merely laughed at her challenge. "You needn't bother with further descriptive terms. I'll settle for 'stud.' Some men might even consider the term a compliment," he reflected.

"Suit yourself," Reva muttered.

He sipped his amber-gold drink without further comment. Reva was annoyed to find that her hand trembled when she lifted her wineglass to her lips. "Shall we get on with our business discussion?" she finally asked briskly.

He tilted his head. "Your sign over the sidewalk is in violation of the lease, you know."

"Yes. I discovered that to be true when I checked over the archaic fine print in the agreement. Fortunately I don't have any unsanitary spittoons sitting around or you could also get me on that."

He merely laughed again, still unperturbed. "An agreement is an agreement," he reminded her, "no matter how inconvenient the details may be."

"I'm submitting a bill to the company from a repairman who worked on the wiring. The lease also says the landlord pays for such repairs."

"We'll live up to our half of the agreement," he agreed. "I'm sure you realize this points up the need for modernizing the electrical system?"

"I've never doubted that need."

"Good." He smiled brilliantly and in an easy, chatty tone of voice went on to talk about plans for the building. It appeared there would be no problems getting the necessary permits for the renovation. The large parking area that came with the building already satisfied that important requirement for a commercial project. A roof top restaurant was being incorporated into the plans. They had considered installing a glassed-in elevator on the exterior of the building to provide separate access to the restaurant, but had decided that would not be in keeping with the historical nature of the structure. Now they were considering one of the elegant, old-fashioned cage-type elevators. In the basement, the construction superintendent had discovered a walk-in safe containing an unexpected—and unexplained—cache of six old-fashioned, claw-footed bathtubs in perfect condition.

In spite of her anger and frustration with Drake, Reva found herself pleased with the plans and intrigued with discoveries about the old building. At least that proved her interest in restoring the building wasn't totally selfish, she thought, feeling virtuous. She was glad the building was being preserved, even if her business would be elsewhere.

Drake appeared in no hurry to get down to the fine details of the business conflict between them. A well-dressed couple in their early thirties stopped by the table, and Drake introduced them as friends from Portland. If they noted Reva's inappropriate attire, they were too well-bred to show it.

"Reva runs a little shop called Cheese 'n' Stuff down in Razor Bay," Drake said, enlarging on the introduction. To

Reva's surprise he also added, "You should stop in there while you're over here on the coast. The shop has an excellent selection."

"We'll do that," the smartly dressed woman agreed.

Reva groaned inwardly. Why would anyone come to the shop of someone who looked the way she did just now, like a fugitive from a garage sale?

They chatted a few moments longer and then moved on. Reva grudgingly thanked Drake for the small plug for her business. Under the circumstances, she wasn't sure she cared to have anyone know she was associated with Cheese 'n' Stuff.

"You're welcome." He leaned toward her across the small table. "Reva, in spite of what you seem to think, I'm not out to destroy your business. It's just that—"

"I'm in the way," she finished for him. "An unfortunate impediment in the pathway of progress."

"A most lovely and desirable impediment," he said softly.

His eyes, rich and deep as brown velvet in the dim light, trapped hers. She felt enveloped by the gaze, wrapped in the luxuriant depths of it. There was warmth there . . . and laughter . . . and desire . . . She realized her hand was wrapped in his, too, his thumb stroking her wrist in a sensuous tryst with her fluttering pulse beat.

"I—I have to be going." She felt oddly helpless, as if some irresistible force were tugging her into unknown depths. "If we're going to get the matter of the lease settled—"

"We'll have dinner first," he said decisively.

"I'm hardly dressed for the dining room!"

"True," he agreed, but his roving appraisal was more amused than critical. "Perhaps you were planning mangled egg sandwiches and another roll in the sand?" he suggested wickedly.

"No!"

"Then perhaps we could settle for letting room service send something up to my—"

"No!" she repeated, even more emphatically. She took a deep, steadying breath. Why had she let herself be drawn into this ridiculous conversation? "Let's just get on with our discussion of the lease." She made a deliberate point of glancing at her watch. "I have another engagement this evening."

"You do?" It was the first thing she had said that appeared to shake Drake's unflappable composure. The brown-velvet eyes hardened to a spiky glitter. "What kind of engagement?"

"That's personal."

"Date with your 'very close male friend'?"

She regarded him coolly. It was none of his business, of course, but why not tell him? "Yes. So I really haven't time to—"

"And what will he do if you're late?" Drake inquired negligently. "Come searching for you with murderous fire in his eyes? Challenge me to a duel?"

"Don't be ridiculous." Reva had difficulty keeping her voice at a normal level. He was making a joke out of her date with Mark. "Mark is very patient and understanding, obviously not virtues you possess."

At some point her wineglass had been refilled, though she was uncertain just when. She wrapped her hands around the stem and waited tensely for Drake to make some humiliating remark about the nature of her date with Mark, considering her present attire.

Instead he said, "I can be patient, even understanding, if the situation warrants it." When she made no comment, he repeated Mark's name thoughtfully, rolling it around as if tasting it from all angles. "Mark who?" he suddenly asked her.

"Crossman," she answered before thinking better of it.

"Crossman," Drake repeated. He sounded as if he were filing the name away for future reference. "Tell me about Mark Crossman."

Reva was about to refuse, but again she asked herself, why not? Why not tell Drake McQuaid exactly what a wonderful person Mark really was? Carefully she did just that. In detail.

"Mark is a math teacher at the local junior high. A very good teacher. He has a marvelous rapport with his students.

My son Brian is very fond of him. He's all the things Brian's real father is not. He's reliable and trustworthy and sensible. He's not always running off on some wild goose chase he thinks will make him rich. He's patient with Brian. They do things together. Athletic events. Building model airplanes. Playing chess.

"His wife was killed in a car accident a couple of years ago, not long after they moved to Razor Bay from the Midwest. He has a daughter, Jade, two years older than Brian. In fact, I met Mark through his daughter when I temporarily filled in for a sick friend as an assistant Girl Scout leader. Jade is a lovely girl and I'm very fond of her. I—I always wanted a daughter."

"Well, well. Mark Crossman sounds like a veritable paragon of virtue. And your two families fit together like a pair of old shoes, don't they? How come you haven't already married this made-to-measure husband?"

"I—I'm considering it." Reva's gaze, which had been fixed defiantly on him, dropped uneasily. She toyed with the wineglass, feigning an absorption in the silvery shimmer of liquid.

"You've listed all Mark's marvelous assets as a father," Drake observed, "but you haven't told me much about Mark as a man."

Somehow Reva felt on less solid ground, and then she berated herself for disloyalty. Mark had any number of excellent qualities as a man, not the least of which was that he was decidedly the marrying kind.

"He's very intelligent, of course," she began. "I can't begin to understand all the things he does with math. He's quiet . . . unassuming." She realized with distaste that a defensive note had crept into her voice, and she fell silent, frowning slightly.

"Loyal, dependable, and faithful," Drake mocked. "But I don't hear you mentioning anything about his attributes as a lover."

Reva's eyes shot up to meet his. "Not all women are attracted to the type of man who parades a—a brazen sexuality!" she said, flaring.

"The 'stud' type," he suggested laconically.

"Yes, if you want to put it that way!"

He leaned across the table and traced the line of her jaw with a forefinger. She felt as if the touch branded her with a moving thread of hot scarlet. The amusement had left his face, and the candlelit shadows emphasized the bold sculpture of his cheekbones. "Reva, Mark Crossman might indeed fulfill your son's needs for a father, but can he fulfill *your* needs?" The words were no more than a whisper, but they echoed through her mind, reverberating over and over— your needs . . . your needs . . . your needs . . .

Distraught, Reva caught his hand to stop the sensuous whisper of his fingertips against the vulnerable curve of her throat. She moistened dry lips and swallowed convulsively. She had the dizzying feeling he had put into incriminating words something of which she had long been vaguely aware but had refused to face squarely.

"You need a man you love heart and body and soul," he pursued with soft relentlessness. "A man who loves you with the same depth."

"That—that's foolishness. Adolescent fantasy." Without her conscious thought, her hand tightened around his, the fingernails biting into his skin.

"Is it?"

She looked at him with wide eyes. Her mind felt drugged, slowed to a sluggish crawl. It was the wine, she thought thickly. She'd had too much wine. She clutched at the thought, in spite of the contrary evidence of the second glass still almost full in front of her. She was vaguely aware of background music, of voices and people moving around, but her senses were targeted on the point of contact between them.

"Have dinner with me."

She shook her head, trying to break that powerful spell. "No, I can't. Really I can't."

"Then meet me after your date with Mark."

She caught her breath, stunned by the audacity of the suggestion, and shocked by the split-second temptation it aroused in her before she snapped out a vehement rejection.

"No! How dare you suggest that?"

"But you're not spending the night with him."

It was true, of course, but somehow Reva was annoyed that Drake was so positive. "What makes you think that?"

"You considered the idea for a moment." He sounded wickedly self-satisfied.

Yes. Just for a moment the thought had raced through her mind that after the drive-in movie she could return here. Good Lord, what was *wrong* with her? She realized his hand was still curved around her throat and his fingers spread through her soft tousle of curls. She jerked her head away and replaced his hand firmly on the table.

"I don't know just how it happened, but our conversation seems to have strayed from my purpose in coming. Now about the lease—"

"Will you forget the damned lease? If you won't meet me tonight, then see me tomorrow."

"I'm working at the store tomorrow."

"Tomorrow night. We'll go somewhere and dance."

"Can't you get it through your head that I'm telling you no?" Reva demanded wildly. "No, no, *no*. I don't want to see you again. You're not the type of man I find . . . admirable."

"You're not attracted to me?"

"No!"

"Liar." He breathed the word on her as if it were a caress, not an epithet. She closed her eyes, reeling under the sensuous force of it. Then he smiled lazily, as if knowing he had branded her with the truth. "Reva, don't you think it's time we faced the attraction between us like adults instead of playing childish games?"

"*You* may be playing games," Reva said grimly, "but I am deadly serious. If you think I'm here tonight because I find you so irresistibly attractive, you're very mistaken. I'm here only because the future of my business is at stake, and this appeared to be the only opportunity I'd have to discuss the lease with you."

She had finally angered him. But the momentary surge of satisfaction this brought was immediately submerged in a sudden jolt of apprehension. A smile returned to his face, but there was a hard glitter of ruthlessness in his eyes. She had the sinking feeling that she was the fluttery sparrow and he the cat who had been toying with her. Now he was through playing, and ready to move in for the kill.

He crossed his arms. "Very well. The lease. Although I'm not sure there is anything to discuss."

What did he mean by that? She took a steadying sip of wine. "We have to discuss the amount Century Development is willing to pay to buy out my lease. The lease has two years yet to run, so—"

"Why should Century Development buy you out? You violated the lease," he reminded her coolly. "Didn't you read the letter? We're declaring the lease null and void because of your violation."

Reva stared at him in shocked dismay. Yes, she had read the letter. Repeatedly. Perhaps, in some corner of her subconscious, she had recognized that it meant Drake's earlier offer to buy out the lease was no longer open, but her conscious mind had refused to acknowledge that disastrous possibility. She had clung to the thought that *something* was salvageable financially.

"You're saying you can just toss me out?" she asked incredulously.

"I suppose you can argue it in court, if you care to."

"That isn't fair!" He knew she hadn't the financial resources to fight him in court.

"You know the old saying—all's fair in—"

Reva jumped to her feet. "You can't throw me out if I'm not in violation of the damned lease!"

"Reva, calm down." He grabbed her left wrist. "I didn't mean—"

He broke off, warily eyeing the half-full glass of wine still clutched in her right hand, evidently remembering the earlier result of her temper.

"The sign will be down by tomorrow," she said grimly. She let him eye the poised wineglass a moment longer, then carefully set it on the small table.

"That's better." He released her wrist cautiously, as if

he half expected her still to turn on him with savage claws. "Now if you'll just sit down so we can talk reasonably—"

"Sorry. I have to see a man about a sign." She whirled and stalked away from the table. Behind her she was aware that he was fumbling for his wallet to pay the bill, and at the door her dignified stalk broke to a frantic dash.

Moments later she was on the two-lane highway headed back to Razor Bay, flinging her little car around the dangerous coastal curves in flagrant haste. At the house she raced to the phone, leaving the front door wide open in her rush to call the company that had erected the sign. She looked up the number, dialed, and then groaned as a recorded voice announced that the company was closed for the weekend. The caller could leave a message at the sound of the beep, the voice advised, and the call would be returned on Monday.

She couldn't wait until Monday.

She tapped her fingers impatiently on the phone book. There were no other sign companies in Razor Bay. But surely the sign couldn't be all that difficult to tear down, could it? Two men had put it up. She and Mark could take it down!

Quickly she dialed Mark's familiar number and rapidly explained to him what had happened and what she wanted to do. There was a short silence at the other end of the line, broken only by a murmur of television voices in the background.

"You mean you think the two of us should rush down there and tear the sign down tonight?" Mark doubtfully repeated what she had just told him as if he couldn't quite believe she meant it.

"Yes!"

"Hon, do you realize how late it is? Jade is already in her pajamas."

"We'd have been out hours later than this if we'd gone to the drive-in," Reva argued impatiently. "It won't take more than a few minutes to get the sign down. I think there are just a few bolts holding it up."

"Couldn't it wait until morning?"

Reva hesitated. She wanted the sign down *tonight,* but she supposed it could wait until morning. "You'll help me do it first thing in the morning then?"

"Hon, don't you think you should consider this situation a little more carefully?" Mark asked soothingly, expertly backtracking. "You're all excited now—"

"Of course I'm excited. The company is threatening to throw me out of the building without paying me a dime!"

"They surely aren't going to take any further action before Monday," Mark pointed out reasonably. "By then you can get someone from the sign company to remove the sign. That would be the safest way, and they can also do it without damaging it."

At this point, Reva didn't care if the sign was smashed to toothpick-sized slivers. She just wanted it *down.* And then just let Drake McQuaid try to get her out of the building, she thought grimly. She'd live up to every letter of the lease and he could take his damned threats and harassments and buy-out offers and stuff them in one of his claw-footed bathtubs.

"You don't want to help me then?" Reva's forefinger was poised to break the connection.

"It isn't that I don't want to help you," Mark said, hedging. "It's just that I think you're acting too impulsively. There are a number of factors to consider here. If you'll calm down and think this through—"

"Mark, there is nothing to think through!" She slammed the receiver down. There were always "factors to consider" when Mark made a decision. Mark pondered all angles. She could admire this in most instances, and it was probably unfair to fault him now for being cautious, but sometimes it seemed to her that his consideration of all factors was a kind of intellectual procrastination that simply avoided taking decisive action.

And right now, Reva's jittery fury demanded *action*, not cautious consideration.

She waited a few moments, thinking he might call back

and say he'd help her, but the phone remained frustratingly silent. He was no doubt giving her time to follow his advice and calm down.

No way, Reva thought resolutely. That sign was coming down, and it was coming down tonight! She went to Bax's old tool drawer at the bottom end of the kitchen cabinet. She had no concrete idea of how to remove the sign alone, but she snatched up hammer, pliers, screwdriver, and several wrenches. The tools made metallic clinks and clunks when she tossed them into the car.

She felt a fresh indignation when she reached the store and stared up at the sign. The marquee-type roof to which it was attached extended out over the sidewalk, yet her sign must not! She supposed that at some time in the long-gone past there had been some logical reason for the restriction, but it made no sense now.

Yet that was beside the point. The sign had to come down. At least she was suitably dressed for the task, she thought wryly. She just wished she had paid more attention when the men were hanging the sign.

The first step, of course, was to get up there. She unlocked the store door and made her way past the dimly lit counters to the back hallway where a ladder was stored. It was a heavy, awkward thing to handle, and she was panting by the time she got it leaned up against the building under the extended roof. Now she wished she had thought to bring a flashlight. The streetlights cast a harsh glare over the empty sidewalks, but under the roof the sign itself was in shadowy darkness.

She climbed the ladder cautiously. It felt reasonably secure. But when she reached back and groped for the sign, she found she couldn't reach it. She had to climb down, wrestle the ladder into a new and decidedly less secure position against the sign itself, and climb up again.

But this time she got the first hint of success. Running her hands along the top of the long wooden sign, she found it was attached to the supporting beam behind it by long bolts. She had only to unscrew the nut on each bolt, remove the bolts, and eventually the sign would fall when all the bolts were out.

She went down, got a wrench from the car, and once more clambered up the ladder. It had, she thought uneasily, all the stability of one of the sand castles she and Brian sometimes constructed on the beach.

She was still on the first bolt, trying to get the hang of using the heavy, awkward wrench, when a car pulled up on the street below. She paused, suddenly apprehensive as a car door slammed. Not even little Razor Bay was free of ugly crime.

Then a familiar figure strode into view. The stark street-light turned his hair a gleaming blue-black, and his shoulders had a menacing hulk as he grabbed the ladder.

"What the hell are you doing up there?" Drake demanded as he peered up at her.

"Obviously I'm removing the sign."

He exploded with an oath. "When you weren't at the house, I figured I'd find you here doing some damn fool thing like this."

"Then I'd appreciate it if you'd just go away and leave me to my damn fool task," Reva retorted from the shadowy height of the ladder.

"Reva, come down from there." It was a warning and a command, not a request.

Reva's response was to let her fingers drop the nut that had finally come loose. It pinged on the sidewalk and then rolled into the gutter.

"Reva..."

She hammered on the end of the bolt with the wrench, effectively drowning out whatever he'd started to say.

"You're acting like a child with a temper tantrum!" he raged when she finally stopped hammering.

She dropped the long bolt. It missed Drake's head by bare inches before clattering to the sidewalk. He didn't let go of the ladder, but he made a cautious sidestep, out of the general danger area of falling metal parts.

"Will you please come down here where we can discuss

this rationally?" He gave the ladder a small warning shake that made Reva clutch the sign for support. A car turned off the main street half a block away and cruised slowly by.

"I believe you said there was nothing to discuss," Reva shot back when the car had passed. She considered how to reach the next bolt. With Drake waiting menacingly at the foot of the ladder, she didn't dare climb down. But it was a precarious lean to the next bolt.

Recklessly she leaned and reached for it.

"If you weren't so hot-tempered, you'd have given me time to finish what I started to say at the inn," he told her harshly.

"I'd heard enough." The ladder gave a small, warning *squawk* as the top slid across the board. Reva caught her breath, feeling the unsteadiness beneath her, then simply took a firmer grip and kept working.

"I'd have told you, if you'd given me time, that under the circumstances the company isn't *obligated* to buy you out, since you violated the terms of the lease, but we're still willing to make a generous settlement on the lease." He let go of the ladder and moved around to the other side of it, trying to see her face in the shadows.

"No, thank you. I don't want your 'generosity.' And I'm not giving up my lease. I won't be in violation once I get the sign down. Cheese 'n' Stuff may have to operate without a sign, but the business is staying right here." She emphasized the decision with the ping and clatter of another dropped nut and bolt.

There was something supremely satisfying about the sounds, as there was in the sound of Drake's frustrated oath that followed. She smiled to herself in the shadow of the marquee.

But now there was a problem. The next bolt was out of reach. She had to move the ladder to get to it, and that meant going down into the dangerous arena of Drake's anger. Unless . . .

She jammed the wrench in a back pocket of her jeans, carefully took a firm grip on the sign with both hands, and hooked one foot under a rung of the ladder. Partially supporting her weight by her hands, she dragged the ladder a few inches sideways with her foot. The move worked perfectly! Except that at the last moment, when Reva let her full weight back on the ladder, something went wrong and the ladder slipped sideways.

Ladder and Reva would have crashed to the concrete if Drake had not grabbed the rungs and righted it with a powerful jerk of his arms.

Reva leaned her head against the sign and felt a sudden outpouring of nervous perspiration beneath the clinging T-shirt. Another moment and she might have been in a broken-bones heap on the sidewalk.

"Now will you come down? Before you break your stubborn neck?"

Reva wiped slippery hands on her jeans. "No," she said, verifying his accusation of stubbornness. "I'm not coming down until the sign is down and I'm no longer in violation of the lease."

"Reva, if you won't come down by yourself, I'm going to come up and drag you down." His voice was imperious.

She got the wrench out of her pocket and started on the next nut. She'd gotten the hang of using the wrench now, and the work was going faster. A few more minutes and the whole sign would come crashing down. Somehow she'd managed to divorce herself from the pride she'd felt when the sign first went up. Now there would be a supreme satisfaction in seeing it crash at Drake's feet, knowing his arrogant plan to evict her would crash with it.

She felt the ladder give a little as Drake tested his weight on the first rung. She glanced down. He stood on the rung a moment and then retreated in frustration. He obviously doubted the ladder would hold their combined weight. She doubted it also.

Serenely she proceeded with her task. Another nut and bolt clanged to the concrete. She readied herself to repeat the moving maneuver with the ladder.

He grabbed a chest-high rung as the ladder again teetered precariously beneath her, threatening any moment to crash to the unyielding sidewalk. "Okay," he muttered savagely, "you win."

She looked down, wrench in hand. The harsh streetlight was unflattering to any complexion, but it couldn't alter the sculptured, aristocratically handsome lines of his face. Just now that face wore an angry but stiffly resigned expression.

"I win what?" she asked warily.

"You can keep your store in the building. We'll work around you. I don't know how the hell we'll do it, but we'll manage somehow. Now will you come down before you fall and break your neck out of sheer stubbornness?"

Reva turned around so that she was half-sitting on a rung of the ladder. "Do you mean it? This isn't just some trick?" she asked suspiciously.

"Do you want it in writing?"

"That might not be a bad idea."

He glared at her. "You'll just have to take my word for it."

"No more hassles? No harassments or threats? I can simply conduct my normal business?"

"As normal as will be possible, under the circumstances."

Reva considered that, then bargained one final point. "And the sign stays?"

He sighed, defeated. "Yes. The sign stays too. Now come down before that damned ladder breaks or falls. I don't want your cracked skull and broken bones on my conscience."

Reva started down the ladder, smiling, breathless with the exultant thrill of victory.

And then the ladder fell.

# Chapter Six

THE LADDER SKITTERED SIDEWAYS, then plunged downward. Reva gave a startled cry and tried to jump free of it. Drake still had hold of one rung and he attempted to keep the ladder from falling, but Reva's frantic leap hit him squarely in the chest and shoulders and knocked him backwards.

They went down in a tangle of arms and legs and Reva's shrieks. The ladder crashed and bounced. Reva saw an explosion of multicolored sparks as her head hit something.

They lay there together on the sidewalk, stunned. Reva felt disoriented. Her nose was buried in something woolly. Finally she felt something move. It was Drake. She was sprawled on top of him. She untangled her arms and legs from his. Drake pulled himself to a half-lying, half-sitting position. He blinked and shook his head to clear it, then rubbed his jaw. Now, on her knees beside him, Reva realized what her head had struck.

"Drake, I'm sorry!" she said, gasping. "Are you all right?"

He moved the jaw from side to side, testing it, but made no move to stand up. "More or less. How about you?"

"I'm okay." She touched his arm tentatively, afraid she

**91**

might find smashed bone. "I landed on you instead of the concrete."

"I'm aware of that," he muttered.

"I—I think I hit you in the jaw with my head."

"I suspected you were hardheaded. Now I'm sure of it."

"I'm really sorry," Reva repeated helplessly. Her head didn't actually hurt, but she felt a little dazed. She hoped a suspicious policeman didn't happen along. She doubted she could navigate a straight-line test properly. She was also becoming aware of little twinges of pain here and there: an awkwardly bent finger, a scraped ankle. "I didn't know the ladder was going to fall," she added defensively.

"Any idiot could see the ladder was ready to fall, with you climbing and dragging it around like some demented monkey. Why do you suppose I was yelling at you to come down before you broke your fool neck?" He rotated his shoulders and moved his legs, checking for damage. Evidently there was nothing serious.

*Any idiot,* she echoed in silent outrage. *Demented monkey!*

"I wouldn't have been up there if it weren't for your ridiculous complaints and threats about the sign!"

He scowled. "What you did was the same as blackmail, you know."

"Blackmail!"

"You forced me under duress to give into your demands."

Reva stood up and took an angry step backwards, hands planted on her hips. "And now I suppose you intend to back out."

A muscle in his cheek jumped spasmodically. He pushed himself to his feet and dusted off his clothes. "No, I said you can stay. I don't go back on my word. My lawyer will tear her hair, and the construction superintendent will throw up his hands in disgust."

"Okay, I get the picture. You're doing me an extravagant favor."

"Obtained under duress and by coercion."

"There are all kinds of duress and coercion," Reva told him scornfully. "Mine just happened to work more effectively than yours." She turned and marched toward the ladder. She tried to lift it near the center, the same way she had wrestled it from back hallway to sidewalk, but discovered she was oddly weak and trembling.

Drake shoved her unceremoniously aside and grabbed the fallen ladder.

"I don't need your help!"

"Just open the door and stay out of the way."

Reva hesitated momentarily, then complied. Actually, in her shaky condition, she wasn't too sure she could get the ladder back inside.

He carried the awkward piece of equipment through the store without hitting anything. Reva showed him where to lean the ladder against the wall of the back hallway. Silently they returned to the main entrance. Reva locked the door.

"Thank you for your help. I presume I may now ignore your letter about my violation of the lease?"

He ignored her question. "Get in my car."

"I will not!" She hesitated warily, noting the menacing clench of his fists. "Why should I?" she amended. The question was still belligerent, but cautious.

"Because you're in no condition to drive, and I intend to see that you reach home without causing another catastrophe and inflicting even worse damage on someone else than you did on me."

No condition to drive? Reva started to protest angrily, then thought better of it as she realized she was still clutching the doorknob on the store for support. Her head had begun to throb and her hands were trembling distinctly now that she'd had time to contemplate what she had just done. People had been killed falling to concrete from the height of the sign where she had scrambled around so recklessly!

He waited by his car while she locked the door on hers. On the way, she stopped to retrieve the nuts and bolts scattered on the sidewalk and in the gutter. He gave an exasperated roll of his eyes.

"You said the sign could stay up. I'll have to replace the bolts."

"Don't do it yourself," he advised laconically.

They drove to Reva's house in silence. She sneaked a glance at his rigid profile. She felt a little foolish now. It would indeed have been more sensible to wait until Monday and have someone who knew what he was doing remove the sign.

"Does your jaw hurt?" she asked tentatively.

"My jaw hurts," he agreed. "Also my hip, both elbows, and my pride. I've been in a few brawls in my time, but this is the first time I've ever been flattened by a one-hundred-and-fifteen-pound woman."

"I—I guess there's a first time for everything." Reva's small attempt at humor fell on unappreciative ears.

He turned the car into the driveway at her house. She opened the door and got out, then leaned over to peer back into the car. "I have some aspirin, if that would help." She hesitated, feeling an awkward need to make amends now that she had triumphed. "If you missed dinner, I could fix a sandwich or something."

He tapped the steering wheel as if debating the advisability of coming into close proximity with her again.

"I promise not to drop coffee—or myself—on you."

"Okay," He didn't sound convinced, but he switched off the engine and followed her to the house. Inside, without asking her permission, he headed for the bathroom. He had a streak of dirt on one cheekbone, and the front of his burgundy pullover was smudged.

There was hamburger in the refrigerator. Reva pressed it into two patties, one large and one small, and slid them under the broiler. She put coffee on to brew and then went to the closed bathroom door.

"What do you like on your hamburger?"

His voice was muffled by running water. "Everything."

She returned to the kitchen and prepared buns with hefty layers of tomato, pickles, and lettuce. When he came out of the bathroom his face was clean and he had removed the pullover. The cuffs of his white shirt were rolled back. He had smoothly muscled forearms that were a suntanned bronze under a light covering of fine, dark hair.

He watched her turn the hamburger patties under the

broiler. "I helped myself to some of your aspirin."

"I hope it helps, though I don't suppose it will do much for your pride." She glanced at him and he looked as if he were about to smile. He caught himself before it broke through and scowled instead.

He straddled a high stool at the breakfast bar, feet braced on the wooden rungs of the stool. "What happened to your big date with Mark Crossman?"

"I called and told him I had some things to take care of." She didn't reveal the specific detail that she had asked Mark to help her and he had refused.

The coffee scented the kitchen with an inviting fragrance. Drake went to the cabinets, unerringly picked the right door to find the cups, and pulled two pottery mugs off the row of hooks. He poured the coffee, got a carton of half-and-half from the refrigerator, added cream to one mug for her, and returned to the tall stool with the other.

A man who wasn't helpless in the kitchen was rather nice, Reva thought grudgingly. In spite of Drake's determinedly unsmiling expression, his presence lent a warmth to the room. She topped the hamburger patties with cheese and slid them back under the broiler.

"I'll try not to get in the way when your men are working on the building." she offered.

"You'll be in the way simply by being there," he countered.

"You aren't exactly gracious in defeat, are you?"

His lips twitched and he finally smiled. "I suppose not."

Reva served the hamburgers. They weren't elegant fare, but Drake attacked his with hearty appetite. Reva suddenly realized that she, too, was famished. Their conversation was limited to his request for more mustard, her offer to refill his mug.

Finally he pushed back the empty plate and pulled the coffee mug over in front of him. She was still eating. He watched her with a thoughtful expression on his face until she finished.

"Will you be here on the coast all weekend?" Reva asked finally.

"I'm not sure. So far, my weekend hasn't exactly gone according to schedule."

"Neither has mine," Reva retorted lightly. The sore spot on the top of her head, where it had encountered Drake's solid jaw, still throbbed lightly, but she felt better now that she had eaten. She stood up and reached across the breakfast bar for his plate. He caught her wrist and pulled her around the end of the counter.

"You don't let anyone push you around, do you?" He sounded undecided between admiration and resentment.

"I'm not sure I know what you mean."

He pulled her into the loose vee of his legs draped around the tall bar stool. His hands slid to the back of her waist and locked there, and his gaze played lightly over her face.

"First you take on Century Development's plan to demolish the building and almost single-handedly stop the project cold. Then you refuse to move out peaceably. Now I find I've not only agreed to let you stay but also to let you keep your damned sign."

"That sign isn't hurting anything and you know it."

"True," he admitted. "But you had a lot of nerve sitting on top of your wobbly old ladder in the dark and bargaining with me about it. How come you weren't simply meek and properly grateful that I was letting you stay, instead of demanding more?" His locked hands slid under her T-shirt and touched bare skin at the back of her waist. She had never before been particularly aware of that portion of her anatomy, but she was electrically aware of it now.

She rested her hands lightly on his shoulders, bracing her arms against the slight but insistent pressure that pulled her toward him. "I need the sign. That clause in the lease was ridiculous."

"I admire that," he said, nearly growling, as if the admission came reluctantly. "I admire someone with the nerve and determination to stand up for her rights and not let anyone push her around."

Reva tilted her head quizzically. "Even when the person doing the pushing is Drake McQuaid?" She touched his earlobe and rubbed it lightly between her thumb and forefinger. It had a sensuous softness against her fingertips.

"Maybe then most of all," he muttered. He moved his head up and down against her hand, like some darkly dangerous beast gentled by the feminine touch. She smoothed his mustache with her fingertips, realizing it was something she had secretly yearned to do. It felt softer than it looked. She fought a sudden impulse to dip her head and kiss the mouth beneath it.

"And what would you have done if you were in my position?" she asked instead.

"Probably the same thing you did," he admitted. "Or something equally outrageous. I don't like being pushed around either. Maybe we're two of a kind."

"Are we? First I'm an idiot. Then a 'demented monkey.' Now I'm outrageous. Do all those terms apply to you, too?" Reva asked teasingly. "And whatever happened to all those lovely things you had to say about me earlier?"

"Such as telling you what gorgeous shoulders you have?"

He pushed the scooped neckline of the T-shirt to one side to expose the creamy curve of her shoulder. Slowly and deliberately he leaned forward and pressed his lips to the smooth skin, centering the kiss with a whispery flick of his tongue. The touch sent a tingle shooting across the shoulder and up her throat.

"I've wanted to do that since the minute I first saw you," he whispered huskily. With teeth and lips he nibbled a searing trail across her shoulder and up the side of her throat to her ear. His teeth bit into her earlobe with just enough pressure to send a fiery arousal streaking through her, as if a new nerve pathway had just opened up and led directly to some slumbering core deep within her.

Her arms no longer held him away. She stroked the back of his neck and felt the hard muscles of his thighs close tautly against her hips. His mouth found hers in a sweet-hungry kiss. It had a controlled strength and depth that asked her to share his rising passion, rather than be dominated by it.

She returned the kiss, feeling her own passion building, like slow, deep-moving water gathering strength and weight behind a dam. He pulled her closer, holding her against his solidly aroused contours until her own desire throbbed in unison with his. His hand found her breast and cupped and squeezed until the breast felt heavy and swollen and ripe, and the clothing that separated his hand from her flesh was a frustrating hindrance to them both.

"Reva, I want to hold you . . . feel your skin next to mine . . . love you . . ." He lifted the T-shirt and trailed kisses across the bare skin beneath her breasts.

The power of her need frightened Reva. She had never before felt controlled by her desires, servant rather than master of them. She had a strange, paradoxical feeling of mental weakness combined with raw animal strength and bodily power, like a cat flexing sleek muscles, or a lioness stretching in preparation for lithe pursuit.

She arched her back and let her head fall backwards, denying nothing to his seeking mouth. He kissed the valley between her breasts, and his tongue climbed the creamy peaks on either side of the valley, only to encounter the wispy barrier of ribbon and lace.

"Let's go into the bedroom," he whispered urgently.

"No!" She was almost surprised that the word had escaped. Her mind still had control of her vocal cords . . . but precious little else.

He lifted his head and looked into her eyes, and she saw in their darkly enlarged depths a magnification of her own powerful desire. "Why?" he demanded softly.

"Because . . . I don't know . . ." She felt as if she were out of her depth in the deep, slow-moving current. It was rising around her, even deeper and more powerful, threatening to submerge her in a will more powerful than her own.

"You can't still have some crazy fear or suspicion of me. You won! I think I'm out of my head for giving in to you. Maybe I've let my feelings for you overrule my better judgment." He studied her face as if searching for clues.

"What . . . feelings?"

There was a small moment of hesitation before he said, "I'm not sure. Desire. Need. Hunger. Maybe . . ." Another hesitation. "I can't sort them out when all I can think of at the moment is how much I want to make love to you."

"There's nothing to sort out!" Reva flared. "They're all the same. Sex." She put her hands on his shoulders and locked her arms into rigid bars between their bodies. But his hands clasping the lower curves of her body trapped her pelvis against him and made a mockery of the space she held open between their upper bodies.

"Do you need some promise of undying love before you can enjoy the simple pleasure of sharing the intimacy of a man's body?" he whispered softly. "A man who finds you very, very desirable?"

"No . . . yes . . . I don't know!" She swallowed convulsively. "You're acting as if I owe you something because you're letting me stay in your damned building!"

"Reva, you owe me nothing, but what do you owe yourself? You're a woman, Reva, a beautiful and supremely desirable woman. You want me as much as I want you, but you won't let yourself acknowledge your desire. You're denying—"

"No! I don't want you! I can't make love with you on the basis of nothing more than . . . physical desire."

"Can't you?" he challenged softly.

"No!"

He wrapped his arms around her and kissed her, holding her body with his legs, kissing her so deeply that she felt submerged in him, as if parts of their beings were blended so deeply they could never again be divided and separated. His tongue claimed and conquered her; his hands brought a soaring song to her body. Yet she was aware, too, that there was much, much more that lay beyond this, that a kiss was only a preliminary to complete oneness . . .

"That doesn't prove anything!" she said, gasping when his mouth finally released her. The kiss and commanding embrace had shaken her, but she still had control. "I can't . . . won't . . . ."

He shook his head, smiling a little. "Such a stubborn woman." His voice had a rich, intimately affectionate warmth. "A stubborn, beautiful woman to whom everything must be proven."

He lifted the shirt and slipped it over her head. Her arms felt nerveless, unable to protest in spite of the knowledge that each step pared relentlessly at her resistance. He traced a finger across the upper edge of the bra, into the valley, around the straining peaks still hidden under the veil of blue lace.

It was Reva, who, with a small animal cry, suddenly released the clasp and flung the bit of lace and ribbon aside. She stood before him naked from the waist up, chest heaving, face warm with color. "That was coming next, wasn't it? But it doesn't change anything because I—I'm still in control. Even like this, I still know mere physical desire can be rejected."

"Can it?" His smile was lazy, knowing. "What if..." Without completing the sentence he dipped his head and traced his tongue around the dusky-rose circle at the peak of each breast. He flicked the nipples with his tongue, tiny quicksilver caresses of exquisite delicacy that exploded fireworks of shooting stars behind her eyes. Her lids were closed and her feet braced in an attitude of brave resistance to his sensuous assault, but only that outer shell of resistance was still inviolate. Inside she was turning liquid, melting, her wild desires giving a lie to everything her mouth proclaimed. His mouth encompassed her breast in a final conquering assault, then moved to work the same wicked magic on its twin. His fingertips slid beneath the waistband of her jeans and his thumbs massaged the exquisitely sensitive areas inside the curve of her hipbones.

If he had said anything, voiced any claim of victory, she might still have dredged up some last ounce of resistance. But he said nothing, and his hands and mouth were everywhere, fiery and primitive, sweet and tender... and she was lost. He scooped her up in his arms and carried her unresistingly down the dimly lit hallway to the open door of her bedroom. The tight jeans, which she usually had to tug off, fell away without resistance under his deft grasp.

In moments he was naked beside her on the bed. In the faint light filtering down the hallway, his body looked lithe and sinewy, the muscles streamlined rather than bulging. A band of lighter-colored skin circled his lean hips. He ran one hand down her body in a long stroke from breast to hip to thigh, then repeated the gesture, one long glide overlapping the other as if he meant to leave no inch untouched. Her body undulated beneath the long caresses, like a wave gently rising and falling.

"I like the feel of you," he whispered. "Soft and smooth on the outside, but taut and firm underneath. I like the way your muscles tighten in response when I touch you. I like the eager life within you and the way your breasts fill my hand with softness and then stand at attention." He laughed in soft, sweet delight, and used his lips to tease the already rigid nipples to hard buttons.

Reva felt shy and a little confused. Once her resistance had vanished, she had expected him to make love to her quickly, impatient for satisfaction, but he seemed in no hurry to rush things. He massaged her abdomen with circular strokes, pressing a little more deeply at the lower end of the circle until her body followed the rhythm of his hand, rising and falling with him, unconsciously straining a little farther each time for the intimate touch that was just out of reach. With each circular stroke, her breath came a little faster, her need climbed a notch higher.

He combed his fingers through the shadowy triangle of soft curl that rose to meet his hand. "Is it the same color as your hair?" he whispered. "Do you know I wondered that the first day I met you? When I wasn't thinking about kissing your shoulders, that is."

"You didn't!" She gasped, shocked, but was feeling a wickedly delicious tingle. She'd had a few thoughts of her own that first day!

"Oh, but I did," he assured her. There was husky laughter in his voice, but the words were thickened with desire. "I wondered all kinds of things about you, and now I'm going to explore and discover each answer for myself. We're going to discover each other . . ." He placed her hand on the criss-cross of muscles on his flat abdomen, within that intimate band of paler skin, and she caught her breath at the powerful evidence of his masculine desire.

Tentatively she traced the vertical line of silky hair that crossed the line between sun-darkened and natural skin. She felt the quiver of taut muscle beneath her hand, and this evidence of what her touch did to him was strangely erotic. It filled her mind with all kinds of wild, daring ideas. She leaned over and ran her tongue lightly along that line that separated bronze-tan skin above from paler skin below. She felt his sharply indrawn breath.

"Oh, sweetheart, you're driving me wild," he groaned. He rolled over her, pinning her to the bed beneath his body. "I don't know whether you're more innocent than you have any right to be, or the world's biggest tease."

"I'm not teasing! I want—" She broke off.

"You want what?" he demanded. He thrust his hips against her, hard. "What do you want?" She could feel the hard pressure of his male desire, so near and yet so far away.

"You know . . ."

"Tell me!" he demanded fiercely.

"Love me!" The words were wrenched out of her by a desire stronger than her reluctance to say them. "I want you to love me."

And when she thought she could stand it no longer, when her body ached with the desperate need, he moved over her, beginning with her the age-old climb to fulfillment that knew no equal. He was masterful but tender, agressive but gentle. She felt the wild thunder of his heartbeat, and then her own blended with it in a primitive drum of passion.

He had won, she thought in some far-off corner of her mind. He had proven he could make her want him beyond all reason, could make her beg him to love her. But she felt no sense of loss, no agony of defeat, only a rising exultation. She felt the slickness of perspiration between them, heard the ragged catch of her own breath. Her body moved with his, tentatively at first, then joyously as she felt his delight in her. She felt him come to the precipice, then draw back to bring her with him. And always she was surging higher and higher, climbing an arched rainbow, and instead of merely seeing the colors, she could also feel them—fiery reds and purples smoldering deep within her body . . . flash of warm golden yellow on her skin . . . and then at the very top of the rainbow's arch a sunburst explosion of shattering light and exquisite sensation. And Drake was there with her and he was a part of the explosion, and it melded them into one . . .

Slowly, with delicious languor, she slid down the far side of the rainbow. Her mind felt dreamy, her senses satiated. Once, long ago, in a despair of disappointment over lovemaking, she had secretly, guiltily, tried to fantasize a pathway to the ecstasy that eluded her. And now she was in the midst of a satisfied delight that went far beyond the meager rewards of any fantasy.

"I knew it would be like this for us," Drake whispered. His voice sounded as content as she felt. He lay beside her with one leg draped possessively over hers.

She snuggled into the secure curve of his arm, her head resting on the muscular pillow of his shoulder. She felt no need to talk, no need to try to fit words to what had happened between them. She reveled in the warm closeness, and when she slept her fingers curled trustingly in the dark mat of hair on his chest.

Once in the night they both awoke. Quickly, without preliminaries, because suddenly none were necessary, they came together in a fiery storm of passionate lovemaking. Where before the climb to the top of the rainbow had been leisurely, with Reva lagging a bit behind, this was a rocket climb, direct to the explosive target, and Reva was with him every inch of the way.

She woke in the morning to find him lying on his side, head propped up with one hand. He was tickling her breast with a stray feather from the pillow and watching with interest at the way the nipple firmed in response even as she slept.

She snatched the sheet up to cover the incriminating response. She didn't know if it was his actions that had caused it, but she had wakened already aroused. "What do you think you're doing?" she demanded indignantly.

"I could be performing a scientific experiment," he said lazily. "Testing the responses of the human body and all that."

"I think you know quite enough about the responses of the human body," Reva retorted with a tart good humor. She rubbed a foot up and down his lean leg, liking the sinewy feel of it.

"And then I might just be thinking about making love to you again." He grinned and reached for her. "I had this terrific dream in the middle of the night."

"It was no dream," Reva assured him, the memory still vivid.

"I'm having another dream now," he whispered. "A wide-awake dream." He drew a pattern around each breast with the feather, then whispered it across the curve of her throat.

Reva caught her breath. "What—what kind of dream?"

"About you making love to me."

"I—I don't know what you mean."

He lifted her as if she were no heavier than the feather with which he had been tantalizing her, and then she was looking down into his dark eyes, her breasts just touching his chest as he held her suspended above him.

"I couldn't . . ."

He moved her upward, holding her so his tongue barely touched the tip of one breast and then the other. The touch was maddening, enough to tantalize, not enough to satisfy. She strained closer, but his arms maintained the maddening distance.

"Why are you doing this to me?" she implored.

"Do you want me?"

"Yes!"

"Then you, my sweet little temptress, will have to do something about it." He smiled, seemingly delighted with her frustration, and she wanted to kiss away that knowing smile, but she couldn't reach his lips. He just smiled infuriatingly, waiting for her to make the first move, and she had the dizzying feeling that he could withhold himself from her for as long as he chose.

But she couldn't . . . she'd never . . .

Then her fierce desire overrode her inhibitions and she made love to him with a wild abandon she had never known she possessed, reveling in the strange new sense of freedom, abandoning forever the imprisoning notion that making love was something that a man did *to* a woman. Neither was conqueror or conquered. There was only the sharing . . . the oneness . . . the explosion that fused rather than disintegrated.

They were tangled in the sheets and pillows. Drake covered her face with a rain of kisses, then planted one directly on the tip of her nose.

"I think you've been saving up for me," he said, teasing her in satisfaction.

Her agreement was tremulous. "Maybe I have." She became aware that she was seeing something over his shoulder. The clock. She had forgotten to set the alarm last night. "I have to open the store in fifteen minutes!" she said gasping.

She leaped out of the tangle of arms and legs and bedclothes, and raced for the bathroom. Her morning shower, toothbrushing, and makeup application were among the speediest on record. She ran naked back to the bedroom and ransacked a drawer for fresh panties and a bra. She was just slipping the panties around her trim hips when she glanced at the bed and saw Drake watching her. He had his hands crossed behind his head and a lazy smile on his face.

"Terrific," he commented approvingly. "Strip tease in reverse."

"If you think you're going to just lie there, better think again," Reva warned. "My car is still down at the store, remember? You have to get up and drive me there."

Drake groaned but tossed the covers good-naturedly aside. Broad daylight revealed the magnificent physique the shadows had only hinted at last night. Wide shoulders, lean, taut buttocks, muscular thighs. He walked naked toward the bathroom with easy, unselfconscious grace. With impulsive impishness, Reva could't resist snapping a towel at that leanly muscled rear. He yelped and came after her, snatching the towel from her and looping it around her body to hold her partially clothed figure against his naked form.

Even though they had made love only moments before, there was wicked intent in his eyes, and his male body was ready.

"No, I can't— Honestly! I have to get to work." Then she shook her head and laughed. "You're insatiable!"

"Only for you." His whisper was surprisingly intense. Then he released her and flicked the towel lightly at her bikini panties. "Now get some more clothes on or I'm taking you back to bed again, and Razor Bay will have to get along without its favorite cheese emporium for the day."

Reva hastened to comply before the temptation to do exactly what he suggested proved too strong to resist.

Beth was already waiting at the front door of the store when Reva arrived with Drake at the wheel of the rented car. Reva slipped out without giving him a good-bye kiss. She felt suddenly self-conscious under Beth's curious gaze. Drake's jaw bore a faint tinge of blue-black shadow from his lack of a shave. Reva had the feeling the sparkle in her eyes and the glow of her skin shouted the ecstasy of last night and this morning for all the world to see. Even her hair had an outrageous independence this morning, the curl a madcap tousle that looked as if Drake had just run his fingers through it. She felt deliciously womanly, sensually aware of small sights and scents that she usually missed— the glitter of sunlight on dew-laden trees across the street, the tantalizing scent of bacon frying from the nearby restaurant.

She also, she realized, trying to gather her dignity and take the lilt out of her walk for Beth's benefit, had missed breakfast. Perhaps *that* was why she was so aware of the bacon frying. But she doubted it. Drake had wakened something in her that went beyond sexuality to an awareness of the other small, sensual pleasures in life.

"Did you get your hair cut or something?" Beth asked, looking perplexed. "You look great."

Haircut? Oh no, Reva sang to herself. She'd had an awakening, a new birth, an introduction to the true joys of making love. She wasn't just a mother, she realized with the astonishment of a scientist making some marvelous new discovery. She was a woman! But all she said was a decorous, "It must be this marvelous weather."

The morning was a normal one in the store, busy moments interspersed with breaks that let them catch up. About ten-thirty, Drake came in. He was carrying a fragrant white paper sack from the bakery in one hand and balancing one coffee cup atop another in the other hand.

"What's this?" Reva asked.

He leaned across the counter and gave her a bold kiss on the cheek. "Breakfast. We missed it, remember? And even lovers have to pause and partake of food occasionally." His voice was low, conspiratorial, meant only for her ears.

He had evidently gone back to the inn and shaved and changed clothes. His open-throated knit shirt clung to muscular shoulders and chest, and Reva felt a strangely visceral reaction to the crisp curl of dark hair at the open neckline. She knew the feel of that masculine mat against her breasts . . .

He grinned at her, eyebrows lifted. "What are you thinking?"

"None of your business," she retorted. He just laughed knowingly at the incriminating rise of color to her already glowing cheeks.

Reva left Beth in charge out front and led Drake to the back room. The fast-food coffee—nicely creamed, of course—Drake never forgot—tasted as delicious as the finest custom-ground, and the maple bars and cream-filled eclairs were fantastic.

"Now, about tonight," Drake said briskly. He sounded as if it were already settled that they would spend the night together, and that just the details were to be worked out. Reva thought about protesting. That old, pre-Drake part of her felt as if she *should* protest. But she didn't. There was nothing she wanted more than to spend tonight with him, so why not admit it? Tonight and maybe longer . . . much, much longer.

The thought gave her a funny little wrench inside. He'd made it so plain that he wanted her, found her physically desirable and delightful. She knew he could give her more than she'd ever imagined of the delights of physical rapture. But there were no promises of undying love. Well, she'd accepted that. He'd proven to her he could make her want him passionately without benefit of love. Yet some stirring deep within her warned she could be playing with emotional fire, that love was perhaps not so far distant. Perhaps even now it was creeping in as stealthily as silent fog. Her stomach muscles gave an odd little contraction as she watched the dark dance of his eyes and flicker of his rakish mustache.

"What are you looking at?" he demanded.

"Your mustache." It was true though her thoughts were elsewhere.

"You like that, eh?" He leaned forward and started whispering in her ear all the wickedly outrageous things he intended to do to her with that mustache tonight.

She blushed and laughed, and shook her head helplessly. "You're impossible."

"And you're fantastic." He gave the bed in the storage room a speculative glance, as if considering possibilities, and Reva rushed hastily on to the subject of tonight before he could brazenly put his thoughts into action.

"I could cook dinner tonight," she suggested.

"You're a marvelous cook. But you've already found another way to my heart," he said significantly. "Tonight I want to take you someplace special."

"The inn is the most special place around here and you've already taken me there."

"No... I'll think of something." He kissed her lightly on the mouth. "I'll meet you at your house after you close the store. Okay?"

"Okay."

Drake almost ran into Beth when he opened the storage-room door. Her hand was poised to knock. Beth opened her mouth to say something, then, with a look of surprised comprehension, snapped it shut until Drake was beyond hearing range. Then she cleared her throat.

"There's a phone call for you, Mrs. Jonathan." Her eyes followed Drake's lithe strides across the store. "It's Mark Crossman."

# Chapter Seven

MARK.

Reva felt a jolt of guilt. Even though she had been seeing
Mark for months, she had hardly given him a thought during
or since last night's passionate lovemaking with Drake. A
second jolt followed, this one of apprehension. Mark undoubtedly assumed they would be seeing each other tonight,
and she had just made a date with Drake. More than a "date";
she'd implicitly agreed to spend the night with him. She
picked up the phone, wondering uneasily what to say to
Mark. She didn't want to deceive him, yet she really didn't
care to go into details either. Mark would be utterly shocked
if he knew everything. In fact, she was more than a little
shocked with herself.

"Hi, hon. I thought I should call and tell you we'd better
not plan anything for tonight." Mark went on to say that
Jade appeared to be coming down with the flu or a cold,
and he wanted to keep her in for a day or two.

Reva was sorry to hear Jade wasn't well, but she couldn't
help feeling a surge of relief. She felt as if she'd been given
a brief reprieve. She wouldn't have to face Mark—or herself—with explanations just yet. She offered to come by

and look in on Jade later, and Mark said he'd appreciate that.

Jade was curled up in a big chair watching television when Reva arrived after closing the store. Jade said Mark had gone out to get pizza for supper. She acted listless, but her forehead didn't feel feverish and she wasn't sniffling or coughing. Reva started asking questions. Did her stomach hurt? No. Her head? No. Impulsively Reva threw in some questions that had nothing to do with physical pain. Had someone hurt her feelings? Sort of. Was she angry? A little. And then it all spilled out. While Jade was away, her best friend had found a new best friend, and now the two of them either snubbed and ignored Jade or giggled and snickered behind her back.

Reva put her arms around Jade, the little girl's pain and unhappiness bringing back with startling clarity something very similar that had happened to Reva long ago. "Oh, sweetie, I'm so sorry," she murmured, smoothing Jade's sandy-blond hair. "I think it's something that happens to everyone sometime."

"Daddy thinks it's silly," Jade said, sniffing. "He told me to just go out and play and we could all three be best friends." She hesitated and toyed with a ball of fuzz on the old blanket tucked around her. "I guess that was when I got sick."

So she wouldn't have to go out and face the other girls. Reva knew it all so well—the pain of loss, the bewilderment when a best friend wasn't a best friend anymore, the little cruelties that might seem trivial to an adult but were so important to a child. Perhaps this best friend's betrayal wasn't something that happened to little boys, so when they grew up to be fathers they didn't understand. But Reva understood. She held Jade and rocked her and told her about her own best friend, Janie Halverston, of long ago. She didn't try to minimize Jade's unhappiness and hurt, and they shed a few tears together. By the time Mark came in with the hot pizza, Jade was feeling better, even giggling a bit.

Mark asked Reva if she'd like to stay, but the pizza was a small one—Mark was always thrifty—and Reva declined. She whispered a bit of advice to Mark before she left that Jade was okay, but it would be a good idea to let her be "sick" for a day or two. She gave Jade a kiss and said she'd check on her again tomorrow.

Drake was sitting in the living room when Reva arrived home. Her heart gave a funny little lurch. He looked shamelessly handsome—flashing dark eyes and smile . . . brazen virility . . . so recklessly, breathtakingly sexy. He also, she thought with a small sense of shock, looked totally out of place. The living room had such a comfortably lived-in look, with well-worn furniture, potted plants and family photos and knickknacks, plus a sweet but crude handmade Mother's Day card from Brian, still occupying a place of honor atop the television set.

In the midst of it, Drake had that darkly dangerous look, like a jungle jaguar momentarily prowling a civilized setting, that attracted her and yet sent a shiver up her spine. He wasn't like Mark, the safe and predictable family-man type. The very ordinary, family-oriented quality of the room was such a stark contrast to Drake's freewheeling, bachelor style of life.

"I didn't expect you here so early." Reva tried to quiet the breathless thud of her heart. He was looking at her with narrowed, speculative eyes, as if contemplating hauling her off to bed without bothering with hellos. There was something heady and exciting about knowing he wanted her when she'd done no more than walk into the room. "How did you get in?"

"Any prowler could find that key you have hidden under the flower pot by the back door," he said airily. He crossed the room and kissed her on the mouth. It was a solid kiss rather than a passionate or seductive one, like some arrogant male animal reestablishing possession of his territory. "Okay, let's get going."

Reva kept her arms around his neck. He sounded so businesslike, and she felt a sudden playful urge to tease him. "Go where?" She lifted her mouth to his and sent a tantalizing flick of her tongue around the outline of his lips and then between them.

"Straight to bed, if you keep that up," he said bluntly. He slipped his hands lower, and she was deliciously aware from the hard thrust of his body that it was no idle threat.

She pouted deliberately. "You promised me dinner out first."

He grinned. "You're a tease," he declared. "A wicked, impish little tease. And later I'm going to punish you for it," he threatened.

"How?" she demanded boldly.

"Just get your suitcase, woman," he said, growling.

She noticed her blue overnight bag standing by the door. "I don't understand."

"I packed a few things for you," he said nonchalantly. "We'll fly up to Portland for dinner and stay in my apartment tonight."

"But . . . we can't do that," Reva protested.

"Why not?"

"Because . . . well . . ." She paused, a little bewildered. "Because I can't just go flying off on a moment's notice!"

"Why not?" he repeated. He sounded puzzled, as if he really didn't understand.

"Because . . ." She knew there must be reasons she couldn't do it—duties, responsibilities, the store, Brian, the expense. But as she went through each objection, she realized with a little sense of shock that there really was no reason she couldn't go. Yet it seemed so *frivolous* just to dash off as if she hadn't a care in the world.

"Well?" he prodded.

A surge of recklessness was growing in her, a heady sense of freedom. Why not, she asked herself. Why not fly off for a fabulous weekend with a handsome, sexy daredevil of a man! The very improbability of it made her laugh delightedly. "Why not?" she agreed breathlessly.

She went to the bedroom to freshen up and change her clothes. He followed, standing in the bedroom doorway, and casually watched her strip to panties and bra. Reva felt self-conscious at first, but then she realized he was watching because he took an open and honest delight in seeing her body. And his gaze, as if he couldn't get enough of seeing her, was suddenly a deliciously exciting thing. She had an impulse to do a hip-swinging, bra twirling little dance for him, but she managed to walk sedately to the shower instead.

"I expected you a little earlier," he commented idly over the hiss of water in the shower. "Did you keep the store open late?"

From under the steamy needles of water, Reva briefly explained about Jade, though she didn't go into the details of Jade's little problem. That had been revealed to her in strictest confidence, and she knew how sacred such little-girl confidences were.

When she stepped out of the shower, Drake was ready with a towel. He dried her shoulders and back efficiently. "Did you tell Mark you were going to be with me tonight?" he asked casually as he worked his way down to the curve of her bottom.

"No."

"Why not?"

"It just didn't come up," she answered evasively.

He turned her around and started drying her breasts and abdomen. She was a little embarrassed at the way her breasts responded instantly to what was a purely utilitarian touch. "Standing at attention," as Drake had put it teasingly last night. He dried the triangle of chestnut curl, too, and it also, she thought, had an embarrassingly vigorous glow.

"Are you really thinking about marrying him?"

"Maybe . . . someday." She felt strange. Here she was, naked with one man, discussing the possibility of marrying another. "I—I'd really rather not discuss it."

"You're very fond of his daughter, aren't you?" There was a tone in his voice she couldn't quite identify. Not disapproval, but *something*. A certain reserve, perhaps, as if he were withholding some sort of judgment.

"She's a sweet girl. Mark doesn't always understand her the way a mother would."

He tossed the towel on the bathroom floor and with it seemed to toss away that momentary dark moodiness. He bent and kissed the tip of each breast lightly, bringing them to a pointed rigidity that pleased him. He tapped each with a fingertip in a final little proprietary gesture.

"I'll get dressed," Reva said breathlessly.

He grinned. "You'd better."

They went by the inn and picked up Drake's suitcase, and at the airfield he tossed both bags in the rear seat of the sleek, four-seater plane. A mist was drifting in as they took off from the small county airfield, but moments later they were above the shallow fog. The sinking sun turned it to a pink-gold fleece below them, and then they were heading northeast over the green-forested coastal mountains.

The Portland-Vancouver area was in dusky twilight by the time they reached the metropolitan airport. The bridges over the Columbia and Willamette rivers looked like jeweled necklaces linking the broader expanse of city lights. Drake had left his car at the airport. It wasn't a Rolls, as he had once made clear, but a nicely sporty Jaguar.

They went first to Drake's apartment, on the third floor of an elegant adults-only complex overlooking the city. This time it was Drake who showered, but Reva prudently let him do his own drying. She slipped into the dress he had packed for her, the clingy, bare-shouldered, white crepe she had worn to the inn.

They dined at a restaurant high atop one of Portland's most elegant hotels, then danced, first at a swinging disco, then to quieter, more intimate music at a lounge. Reva felt starry-eyed and breathless, high on the intoxication of his touch and undivided attention, and the slow, secret smiles of intimate promise he gave her every now and then. The moon had risen by the time they returned to Drake's apartment.

Without turning on the lights, Drake took Reva's hand and led her through the dark apartment. She thought they were headed for the bedroom, but instead he took her to the picture window that looked to the east. She caught her breath, spellbound by the beauty of the scene. The city lights were below, jeweled and lovely, but rising in the distance beyond a gulf of darkness was Mount Hood, snow-capped, solitary, serene, putting man's small twinkling lights to shame in its sheer, massive majesty.

They stood in the oblong of moonlight streaming through the picture window, Drake behind her with his arms around her. Reva felt oddly choked up. She could almost understand how a primitive people could worship such grandeur, imbue it with mystical meaning and power.

Slowly, without speaking, Drake turned her around to face him. He kissed the moon-gilded skin of her bare shoulders and throat. Reva stood unmoving, lips parted, as he gently and almost ceremoniously removed her dress and undergarments until she stood there naked in the moonlight. Once she would have felt self-conscious, but not here and now, not with Drake.

He removed his own clothing and then, without ever speaking, made love to her there in the moonlight, with nothing but the padded carpet beneath them as their two bodies joined in perfect union. There was a purity to it, like the clarity of a song sung in perfect pitch without benefit, or hindrance, of accompaniment. When he carried her to the bedroom afterwards, she felt cherished, as precious as some rare jewel to him.

Yet in the morning he was as playful as a young stallion just discovering his sexual powers. He tickled her breasts with his mustache and sent fiery little shivers through her when he explored her navel with his tongue. He played a frivolously erotic game of hide-and-seek with the sheet and her breasts. He invited her wordlessly to be just as playful, and she found herself tickling and laughing and biting playfully in return, teasing him with advances and retreats until he made a reckless lunge for her and they both tumbled to the floor and made love there in a tangle of sheets and blankets. The first time was quick and sharp and explosive, and then he wrapped himself around her and they slept again. The next time was leisurely sensuous, a deep, slow exploration that prolonged the final peak until Reva felt almost deliriously faint, overdosed on pleasure and anticipation until the final soaring moment was both shimmering rapture and exquisite relief.

"Reva, if ever two people were meant to make love, we're the two," Drake told her afterward. There was a rich contentment in his voice that expressed her feeling exactly. He made her body feel lush and voluptuous, totally female, proud that she could satisfy him so totally—and be so blissfully satisfied in return.

"I wish I could purr." She snuggled herself catlike against him. "It's the only way to express how I feel."

There was one small moment of dismay when she went into the bathroom. An elegant, dangling spike of an earring lay on a glass corner shelf. It was a small jolt of reminder that she wasn't the only woman who found Drake McQuaid wildly attractive, and that his passionate lovemaking had experience behind it. He followed her into the bathroom, and his gaze followed hers to the earring. He caught her upper arms lightly from behind.

"The earring may be here," he said gruffly, "but the woman isn't. Not for a long, long time."

"You don't have to explain to me."

"There's nothing to explain. I . . ." He hesitated and his eyes met hers in their mirror reflections, as if he had started to say something and then caught himself. "Let's give *us* a little while, okay? I don't believe in early commitments. Maybe we'll be tired of each other in a week."

"Is that how long your passionate affairs usually last?" she said harshly, suddenly stung by his words.

He just laughed softly. "You're a fighter, aren't you? I think I can see you pulling hair and scratching eyes if some woman went after your man."

"I wouldn't!" Reva cried, aghast. But on second thought, she wasn't so sure. If the man involved were Drake . . .

He kissed her on the side of the throat and then scooped the earring into the wastepaper basket, where it made a nicely satisfying clunk.

"Do you remember who it belonged to?" she demanded, not caring that the question was a denial of her earlier protestation that he need not explain.

"Of course I remember." He scowled lightly. "Reva, there isn't some endless, nameless parade of females through my bedroom. I won't deny I've been involved a few times. But I wouldn't be here with you now if any of them had meant anything really special."

Which also meant *she* didn't necessarily mean anything special, she thought with a brief plunge into desolation. Just another in a long line of weekend playmates...

Then she quickly got control of herself. This was just a fling for her, too, a wildly improbable summertime fling with a man who was too handsome, too sexy, too adventurous. He had too much dash and flair, too much erotic expertise. Drake wasn't husband-father material. He'd been as out of place in her family-style living room as a painting of a nude on velvet. He was an exciting—but temporary—interlude that would never have happened if Brian hadn't been away.

So why not live her temporary fling to the fullest?

She turned to him, eyes sparkling. "You know what? I've never had champagne for breakfast."

His eyes returned the dancing sparkle. "We can take care of that right now."

They had champagne and a caviar omelet for brunch, breakfasttime having passed by while they made love. After wards they wandered through the Portland zoo and delighted in watching the baby elephants. Finally, in late afternoon, they flew back to Razor Bay.

Reva wasn't really surprised when, after taking her back to the house in his rented car, Drake said he had to leave right away. He had to fly to Bend, tonight, in the central part of the state, in order to make an early-morning breakfast meeting there.

He carried her bag into the house and kissed her goodbye. It was a careful, almost chaste kiss, so as not to lead further. Even after a weekend of intense lovemaking, the hunger for each other was still there. He locked his hands behind her back and looked into her eyes.

"I don't want to leave," he said huskily.

She made her return light, paraphrasing what he had said—was it only yesterday?—about lovers having to eat. "Even lovers have to stop and work occasionally."

"I don't know yet just when I can get back here. The construction crew will be working tomorrow, but I also have this other project over in Bend. I'll call you and get back here as soon as I can." But still he didn't release her. "I don't know about leaving you here with that Mark Crossman guy," he said finally.

Reva was astonished. "Mark? Why, Mark and I have never even—" She broke off, flushing a little at the intimate admission, though she doubted that it came as any real surprise to Drake.

"I have the odd feeling that I now know why women have complained all these years about being regarded as nothing more than sex objects," he said reflectively.

Reva felt bewildered. "You'll pardon me if I don't see the connection?"

"Maybe women are turning the old double standard around. Once there used to be two types of women: the kind you brought home to mother and married, and the other you *didn't* introduce to mother or marry. I get the feeling I'm the kind of *guy* you don't bring home to mother." He touched his lips lightly to her nose. "And Mark is. Maybe I'll come back and find you've up and married him."

Reva caught her breath. She was uncertain if he was serious or just teasing her because of the sex-filled weekend they had just shared. Probably the latter, she decided shakily.

"I'm sure there's nothing you enjoy more than being regarded as a good, old-fashioned sex object," she said lightly teasing him, though the thought lingered in her mind that perhaps there was a measure of truth in what Drake said. He was definitely a bit on the racy side to bring home to mother. But then, *her* mother was hundreds of miles away.

He scowled, and there was an almost angry flash in his eyes in response to her comment. Then he grinned and sighed. "I suppose so. Some of us are simply doomed to be sex objects."

"You'll just have to grin and bear it," she advised teasingly.

He kissed her again, on the cheek, and then he was gone.

Reva felt strange after he was gone, not quite certain the weekend hadn't been some erotic figment of her overactive imagination. Had she really done all those wild and silly and passionate things with Drake? Sex really wasn't overrated after all, she thought with a little giggle, wishing she could share the thought with Drake. It really did live up to its enthusiastic publicity—with the right man!

She was jolted back to mundane reality with the ringing of the phone. It was Brian. His tone was accusing for a few moments. He had been trying to call her all day, and she wasn't there. Reva murmured a little explanation, but by then his resentment was forgotten as he rushed on to the purpose of his call. His dad was going to buy him a soccer ball, and there was a question he wanted to ask Mark about getting the right kind of ball. Carefully Reva penciled the question on the pad by the phone, knowing she wouldn't get it right otherwise. Balls and sports were a not-too-fascinating mystery to her, but she knew how important they were to Brian. She promised to get an answer from Mark and call Brian when she had it.

She dialed Mark's number immediately after talking with Brian. She was tense, wondering how to explain her absence last night, but as she talked with Mark she realized with a small sense of astonishment that Mark didn't even know she'd been gone. She had spent the night in another man's bed, made passionate love with him, and Mark hadn't the slightest inkling of it! She didn't know whether to be grateful, angry, or guilty, and wound up feeling a confusing mixture of all three.

Mark didn't know the answer to Brian's question but promised to find out right away. Reva knew he'd do it. Mark was very conscientious and dependable about things like that. He said Jade was feeling much better today, and would Reva like to come over and make some of her good toasted-cheese sandwiches and hot chocolate for them?

Reva hesitated. She really didn't want to see Mark, partly out of a kind of guilt, partly because she wanted to cling to memories of the marvelous weekend as long as she could. Seeing Mark would somehow bring it to a definite close. There was also the feeling that an inescapable aura of sex clung to her, that a glow and a perfume and a sleek satisfaction permeated every inch of her.

But, thinking beyond Mark to Jade's needs, Reva said she'd be there a little later. She was perfectly clean, but she showered anyway, feeling the need to do something about the blatant sexual aura. Then she dressed in her usual faded jeans and old cotton blouse.

Mark didn't seem to notice anything different about her, or to suspect anything. Reva was relieved yet oddly disturbed. It seemed to point up some enormous, unsuspected gulf between them, if she could feel so changed and he didn't even notice.

Reva fixed supper and then the three of them played Scrabble. It was a comfortable, homey evening that more than ever made the weekend with Drake feel like some improbable fantasy.

It was quite possible, Reva thought slowly as she drove home alone later, that she would never see Drake again except in some purely business context. She didn't doubt but that the weekend had been fantastic for him, as it had been for her. At the moment he might even intend to see her again. But there were other projects in other towns . . . and other eager women and a world of fantastic weekends to explore. She reminded herself it was just a fling for her, too, but she couldn't escape an unfamiliar, almost aching sense of loss that went beyond sex to something deeper.

The construction crew was at work on the building Monday morning. The first thing one man did, evidently under Drake's orders, was to replace the bolts on her Cheese 'n' Stuff sign and make it fully secure again. As Drake had warned, there was noise and dust, and she had to clean and dust constantly. Mark came by once and shook his head.

He still thought she'd been foolish for not getting out. He'd gotten an answer to Brian's question about the soccer ball, and Reva relayed the information to Brian Wednesday night.

She heard nothing from Drake. She felt regret . . . relief, a little hurt . . . a little anger. She carried on imaginary dialogs in her head with him, conversations in which she came off cool and witty and devastating. But when she picked up the phone at the store Friday morning and Drake was on the other line, her cool wit evaporated in a burst of sheer joy. Her hand trembled and she felt a fluttery tug inside. Silly nerves, she told herself. But she half suspected it was a tug of sheer sexual arousal brought on by nothing more than Drake's intimately husky voice.

"How do you feel about Shakespeare this weekend?" he asked without preliminaries.

"Shakespeare?" she repeated blankly. A thunderous noise interrupted from upstairs. The workmen were hard at it. She plugged a finger in one ear. "What about Shakespeare?"

"I remember you saying you'd always wanted to see a play at the Shakespearean Festival down in Ashland. I called some friends there and they can get tickets. We can fly down tomorrow, take in a performance at the theater and spend a night with my friends, then fly back Sunday. The theater is doing *Taming of the Shrew* Saturday night. I thought I might pick up a few helpful hints on taming methods," he said teasingly.

"Do you like tame women?" Reva challenged.

"Nope. I prefer *you*," he said complacently. She could hear the grin in his voice. "So, how about this weekend?"

Reva started to protest that she couldn't do it. She couldn't just go flying off . . . Then she stopped the automatic denial in mid-protest. Yes, she *could* do it! She could get Mrs. Parker, the former owner, to come in and oversee the store for one day. She would just fly off to Ashland with Drake!

"What time?" she asked, not bothering with other minor details. When he said he'd fly into the county airfield about ten-thirty Saturday morning, she said she'd be ready and waiting.

"Ready for what?" he asked teasing her in that husky,

intimate voice that sent a tingly reaction through her.

"Anything," she retorted boldly.

And then the time had come, the confrontation she had dreaded and avoided. She had to tell Mark. She knew she could probably get by with the deception for another weekend. She could probably do it by evasion rather than outright lying to Mark. But that wouldn't be fair or honest. When he called later to see if she wanted to go to the drive-in or just watch television that night, she told him she'd like to talk to him. She asked him to meet her at the coffee shop across the street from the store at about two-thirty. He agreed, though he sounded more annoyed than curious about her unusual request.

She ordered the coffees and had Mark's waiting when he arrived. She was relieved he hadn't brought Jade. She hadn't thought to ask him not to bring his daughter, but what she had to say would have been impossible in front of the girl. He slid into the booth across from her and frowned at the dark liquid in his cup. Mark disliked restaurant coffee; he said it was always too strong and bitter.

Briefly, unemotionally, Reva explained about herself and Drake, and that she was flying down to Ashland with Drake this weekend. If the sexual aspect of their relationship hadn't been crystal clear to Mark from her first words, her unambiguous statement about the weekend together finally got through to him.

He shook his head. "I guess I'm—flabbergasted. I find it hard to believe." His blue eyes roamed over her as if seeing her in a new and definitely not complimentary light. "I never thought you were that type of woman. I mean, you made it so plain you considered him some despicable womanchaser. I certainly never thought you'd be attracted to a man like that. I thought you had better sense. And higher standards."

Reva caught her lower lip between her teeth, fighting the urge to rise to Drake's and her own savage defense.

"Are you in love with him?"

"I'm not sure," she answered reluctantly. She had known he would ask that, of course, and that it would be easier to profess some undying love as an excuse for her flagrant behavior. Instead, trying to be honest, she said, "Perhaps 'infatuation' would be a more accurate word at the moment."

Mark made a derogatory sound that combined anger, disbelief, and disgust.

"I'm sorry," Reva said finally, the words more wooden than apologetic.

"He's good-looking, I suppose." Mark's lip curled. "Charming. Smooth-talking." His disdain was supreme.

"He's fun," Reva returned, finally goaded to a defense. "We talk . . . and laugh. He makes me feel happy and alive."

"And I don't."

Reva swallowed. "My feelings for you are . . . different."

"But you do have feelings for me." He sounded scornful of that also.

"Yes, of course I do. And for Jade too."

He sipped the coffee, for once not seeming to notice its black strength. "Well, Reva, I can't say I'm not disappointed in you," he stated disapprovingly. His expression was closed, as if he were smothering his emotions behind a mask, perhaps not even acknowledging their existence to himself. She almost wished he would rage and scream.

Yet that wasn't fair, she told herself. Part of the confidence she had always felt in Mark was in knowing he *could* be relied upon to act calmly and without excited impulse. He never acted without cautiously weighing results first. In any test of husband-father qualifications, Mark would probably score at the top of the heap, yet she was racing off to spend a weekend with a man who probably had no aspirations at all along the husband-father line, much less qualifications for the position.

"I didn't have to tell you about Drake," Reva reminded him defensively. "I could have just sneaked around behind your back to see him."

"I realize that." Mark nodded slowly. "It's one of the reasons I feel our relationship may possibly survive this. You have a basic honesty. I can only hope you'll come to your senses before long. Surely you won't throw away the important relationship you and I and our children have with each other just for a tawdry affair."

Reva straightened, anger filling her. "It isn't a . . . tawdry affair." But her voice trailed off uncertainly as she repeated his disdainful words. *Tawdry affair*. Was that what it was?

Perhaps what she should do was throw herself at Mark, beg him to save her from herself and her own treacherous desires. Beg him to marry her right now, so she couldn't go flying off with Drake on some wild weekend.

It wasn't the knowledge that Mark would never agree to such an impulsive step as a rushed marriage that stopped her from saying the words. She *wanted* to spend this weekend with Drake—wanted it fiercely, savagely! She knew she would ruthlessly crush any obstacles that arose in order to spend the weekend with him. No matter if it was only a temporary, even tawdry affair. She wanted him.

Mark stood up and threw some money on the table for the coffee. "Let me know when you come to your senses," he said tightly. "I'll be waiting. For a while anyway. And then we'll forget this nonsense ever happened."

Reva watched him go, her emotions an uncertain jumble of surprise, anger, and an unexpected feeling that was, she guessed, respect. He was so damned infuriatingly self-righteous in his attitude that her relationship with Drake had to be a "tawdry affair," so scornful of her attraction to Drake! Yet there was a certain nobility about his willingness, albeit a stiff willingness, to take her back after the fling was over and she came to her senses.

Or was it really a holier-than-thou attitude rather than a noble generosity in forgiving her errant ways? If the affair with Drake ended—as it surely must—would Mark years from now throw it up to her? Would he make her pay in a hundred little ways for her betrayal?

No. If Mark said he'd forget it, that was exactly what he would do. Mark was dependable.

But there was a separate little part of Reva somewhere deep inside that looked on with a kind of horror at the thought of being married to Mark years from now, even if her misdeeds were long forgotten. Living with his studied, stuffy ways, never being playful, foolish, or impulsive.

Doing nothing—neither battling nor loving—passionately.

Reva's feelings were still mixed as she made her way slowly back to the store. Mark had reacted more or less as she had expected him to, except for the surprise of that stiff offer to take her back when she "came to her senses" and the fling was over. Could she have been as generous if the tables were turned, and Mark the one bewitched by some sexy new playmate? She would be taken aback if he had done something like that, she realized thoughtfully, but she would not be devastated. As Mark had not been devastated. So what did all that mean?

She felt she owed Mark some deeper thought on this subject, but the store was busy when she returned. Then she had to contact Mrs. Parker about working there tomorrow and straighten out a problem with the bank. Then she ran impulsively down to Jill Anderson's dress shop and bought a softly feminine heather-blue skirt and jacket to wear to the outdoor Elizabethan theater in Ashland. Boldly she added a daring black and silver nightie to take the place of her usual cotton pajamas, causing Jill's eyebrows to vault upward in speculation.

That evening Reva washed her hair, called Brian, who was excited about a sailboat ride his dad had planned for this weekend, and did a load of laundry. She zipped through a quick housecleaning and packed.

She was waiting at the small noncommercial airfield the next morning when Drake's plane appeared in the northeastern sky. It was a black dot at first, then a winged shape circling overhead in the landing pattern, and finally Drake was climbing out, unbelievably handsome, smiling, the wind ruffling his hair. She couldn't quite believe he had flown in for the sole purpose of swooping her up and carrying her off with him.

But it was true, as he made abundantly clear by picking her up and swinging her around in an exuberant circle and then planting an unabashedly sexy kiss on her mouth.

"It seems like a month since I've made love to you," he told her. "I hurt all over wanting you."

"No doubt you're planning to make up for lost time this

weekend," Reva said teasingly. Demurely she added, "Of course *I'm* only interested in seeing the performance of a Shakespearean play."

"Unless we sneak in a little loving first, I'm not apt to know if they're performing Shakespeare or Micky Mouse," he said, growling. He held her at arm's length, his expression severe. "Woman, do you know what you *do* to me?"

"I know what you do to me," Reva returned. She'd intended the words to be light and impish, but instead they came out almost tremulous, because he did do something to her—something she was suddenly afraid went far beyond mere physical arousal and touched the most vulnerable recesses of her heart.

Moments later they were flying over the mountainous landscape of southern Oregon, with a bit of a detour to view the incredible blue jewel of Crater Lake cradled in an old volcanic cone. Then they dropped down to land at the small town of Ashland, with the green-forested Siskiyou Mountains looming in the background.

Drake's friend, Matt Wyland, came when Drake telephoned to tell him they had arrived. Matt, who was a history professor at the local college, had a distinguished-looking silver-gray beard, a vivacious wife named Vivian, and five children. Each child, it appeared to a rather overwhelmed Reva, had one or more pets plus an assortment of friends. The plumbing had just sprung a leak and flooded the guest room. Reva found herself occupying a bedroom with an indeterminate number of little girls, cats, stuffed animals, and a stereo blaring loud music. Drake looked a little dismayed as he was whisked off to share the boys' room.

"I'd forgotten Matt's life was so damned domestic now," Drake said, groaning, when he and Reva got back together again a few minutes later. The last time Drake had visited Matt, Matt's ex-wife had had custody of his two kids, and Vivian's three were with her ex-husband for the summer. It had been a sane, *adult* weekend. Now all the kids were in permanent residence in the Wyland household, and Drake's obvious opinion was that it was a madhouse. He suggested surreptitiously that he and Reva hie themselves off to a motel for the night, but Reva didn't see how they could do it without being terribly rude, and he sighed and agreed.

They did escape the bedlam to take a hand-in-hand stroll through Lithia Park, where geese and ducks floated serenely in the quiet pools of water, only occasionally losing their dignity to squabble over bread crumbs tossed by onlookers. They tasted the famous mineral water from the fountain, puckering a little at the strange taste and then laughing together. The trails by the stream through the park were sun-dappled and peaceful. Here and there some student from the nearby college pored over a book or, more often, gazed dreamily into the blue sky and cream-puff clouds overhead.

The four adults went out for dinner without the children, but there was the interruption of the baby-sitter calling in a panic to say she'd counted heads at bedtime and one child was missing. Vivian finally got everything straightened out. A visiting girl had developed a sudden case of homesickness and gone home. But by then Vivian's veal scallopini was cold.

The performance of *The Taming of the Shrew* on the authentic outdoor Elizabethan stage was marvelous, however. A skyful of stars glittered overhead and the night air was brisk and tangy, carrying the actors' voices perfectly. The costumes were superb, the "shrew" delightfully tamed. Even Drake seemed temporarily to forget his frustration at being able to do no more than hold Reva's hand. After the play, she could tell he was ready for further action, but Matt and Vivian had to get home to relieve the baby-sitter. They all wound up just drinking brandy-laced coffee in the kitchen, and even that was interrupted by a child wailing about an upset stomach.

If ever there was an advertisement against the domestic life, Reva sighed ruefully, this was it. She saw Drake take a detour by the living-room sofa and knew he was contemplating a daring rendezvous later, after everyone was asleep. She also knew the sofa was occupied by a lanky visiting boy who had been banished from the communal sleeping room because he snored. Drake settled for a disgruntled kiss.

The next day there was a drive up Mount Ashland in the Wylands' roomy van, followed by a picnic on the lake at which an incredible amount of take-out chicken was consumed. By that time Drake had evidently given up on the potential for any amorous activity this weekend and joined the kids and dogs in a wild Frisbee game. Afterwards he gave the giggling younger children rides on his shoulders and finally took the three older children up for a quick plane ride before he and Reva had to leave.

The weekend had been marvelous fun for Reva in spite of feeling Drake's groaning frustration at the various roadblocks that limited them to an occasional kiss or stolen caress. There was, in fact, a certain delicious tension in the delay and knowledge that Drake could hardly wait to get his hands on her. She "accidentally" touched him intimately under the table once and had the sweet satisfaction of hearing him give a small groan of torment in response.

They flew back to Razor Bay in the face of a blazing sunset, and the small airfield was in soft dusk when they arrived. Reva couldn't resist a final bit of teasing when Drake helped her out of the plane.

"Thank you for a lovely weekend," she said primly. "I know you have to be on your way, so—"

"I'm staying the night," Drake said, growling. "I may have to get up at four o'clock in the morning to make it to my first appointment in Portland on time tomorrow, but I'm staying the night. I think you enjoyed seeing me suffer all weekend," he added accusingly.

Reva just laughed, knowing nothing could have kept him away from her bed tonight. And knowing just as well that, if he'd really started to go, she'd have wrapped her arms around him and begged him to stay.

They were no more than inside the house when Drake swooped her up in his arms and carried her off to the bedroom.

"We haven't even eaten dinner," Reva protested laughingly, with her arms flung around his neck.

"The only thing I'm hungry for is you. And I'm starved, do you know that?" He made a ferocious nip at her throat.

"Starved for the feel and scent and taste of you! I want to kiss every inch of you. I'm going to love you till every teasing little bone in your body is too limp to tease any more!"

He practically tore off her clothes, flinging them to chair and floor in wild abandon, rough with hunger for her. Reva gloried in his needy haste and the trembling pleasure his hands took when he finally ran them over her eager, naked body. And then she helped him rid himself of the barrier of his clothing, pulling and tugging at stubborn buttons and a recalcitrant zipper.

He was beautiful, she thought with a kind of awe when he was as naked as she—long, clean-lined muscles, taut abdomen, gloriously aroused manhood, triangular slant of broad shoulders to lean hips. His body was as perfectly proportioned as a sculpture of some mythical god. But above the sculptured body was the wickedly flashing smile of one very human male with devilish intent in his darkly smoldering eyes.

The roughness turned to sweet, sensual tenderness as he settled into her with a small sound of satisfaction, like a wanderer returning home. Then he surprised her. She had expected his need to be so great that his lovemaking would be frantic with haste, but once united with her he seemed momentarily satisfied, blissful in the totality of mere contact. He took a sensual delight in prolonging the pleasure of making love rather than racing headlong to the final goal. He kissed her mouth and shoulders and throat and breasts. He explored with her the delights of changes in pace and depth. She nibbled at his earlobes and chest and invented new ways to roll and rotate her hips and delighted in his answering inventiveness.

There was a glorious freedom to making love with Drake, Reva thought dreamily as they drifted momentarily on a quiet plateau of motionless pleasure. She felt uninhibited, unrestrained, free to give full play to her imagination. She was aware that new and exciting vistas lay beyond, that her imagination was yet in its infancy. With Drake there was both passion and playfulness, the thrill of conquest and delight of submission, toughness and tenderness, give and take. Loving and being loved.

And just then the moments of silent, motionless union gave way to a wild burst of action, and she received his thrusts eagerly, yielding and claiming and demanding and giving, until that calm plateau was left far behind as they climbed the mountain to dizzying heights among the stars . . . and created a new galaxy there, an exploding universe between and within themselves, for themselves alone.

A long time later Drake gave the soft groan of a man weak with a surfeit of pleasure. His weight was still heavy on her, but Reva felt no urge to move. The weight felt comfortable, tangibly solid and reassuring.

"Do they give awards for best lovers of the year?" she murmured contentedly. "We'd surely win."

"Make that best lovers of the century." He kissed her nose and his voice was husky when he added, "I suppose there's nothing new under the sun in the way of making love, but with you it all seems so wonderfully fresh and new, as if we are the very first explorers and discoverers of something wonderful."

Reva rubbed her nose against his. "How about discovering some food in the kitchen? Or would you rather just make love again?" She rubbed her body against his with an easy seductiveness.

"Insatiable woman," he muttered.

Reva just laughed delightedly. At the moment she felt marvelously, luxuriantly satiated, but she knew he could, if he wanted, bring her to delicious arousal again. Or she could do the same thing to him. She lay there, thinking about the choice between eating and making love again, and eating was running a distant second.

The phone rang. Reva listened to it dreamily, not really wanting to talk to anyone. Oh, but it could be Brian, she realized. She leaned across the bed. Drake's hand covered hers, holding the ringing phone down for a moment longer.

"If that's your friend Crossman, you're busy," he warned. Narrow-eyed, he added, "Permanently."

Reva's heart gave a thunderous lurch. *Permanently?* Then he grinned and lifted the phone to her ear.

"Hello."

"Reva, for God's sake, where have you been?" Bax exploded. "Brian is missing."

# Chapter Eight

BAX RACED ON to say that Brian had been gone since yesterday afternoon. Bax had planned to take him sailing, but the plans had fallen through. Brian had disappeared while Bax was out having a few beers with some friends. The police had been notified, and Bax and Mikki had searched everywhere they could think, but without success.

Most of Bax's explanation fell on numbed ears. All that penetrated Reva's mind was the basic horrifying fact that Brian was gone, missing since yesterday. A series of blood-curdling images clicked instantaneously through her mind. Eight years old, wandering alone. *Anything* could happen to him. She cut into Bax's acrimonious tirade about not being able to get hold of her with the brusque comment that she would be there as soon as possible.

She leaped out of bed the moment she set down the phone, telling Drake what had happened as she raced from bed to closet to bureau drawers with frantic haste. If she started driving immediately, she could reach San Jose by morning. Oh, Lord, if anything happened to Brian... She felt sick to her stomach, so shaky that she spilled a drawer on the floor. She had to *hurry!*

Drake grabbed her wrist. "Reva, stop it."

She whirled on him, eyes blazing as she wrenched her wrist away from him. "Let go of me!"

"Reva, stop! Think with me for a minute," Drake commanded. "If you drive all night, you'll arrive too exhausted to do anything." Swiftly he outlined an alternate plan. They would stay here tonight and take off in the plane at first light of dawn. They would arrive in San Jose no later than if she drove all night, and they would be fresh and in good shape to search for Brian.

Reva finally calmed down enough to consider his plan rationally. It made sense. "You'd do this for me?" she asked wonderingly, knowing he had a heavy business schedule and appointments to keep.

He wrapped his arms around her. "You have no idea what I'd do for you," he said huskily.

Drake immediately made several phone calls, contacting his secretary at her home with instructions to cancel appointments, calling a subcontractor on the Bend job, delegating authority to a subordinate on a bid proposal. Reva contacted Mrs. Parker and arranged for her to take care of the store again. Then, out of sheer determination to be in physical and mental shape to do her best for Brian tomorrow, she forced herself to eat a sandwich and sleep.

They ate a hurried breakfast next morning and by daybreak were in the air, following the rough northern California coastline to the San Francisco area, then angling across the bay to San Jose. Some part of Reva's mind took in the beauty of the flight—glorious sunrise, forested mountains to the east, blue-gray ocean to the west, graceful line of the Golden Gate Bridge. But in the face of her awful terror for Brian, none of it mattered.

Reva telephoned Bax as soon as they landed in San Jose. Mikki answered on the first ring. She said Bax was out searching. Mikki was staying by the phone in case Brian called home or the police turned up some information. She offered to come to the airport to get Drake and Reva, but Reva thought her idea of staying by the phone was a better plan.

Drake rented a car and they started driving around, but

within minutes Reva was in tears, overwhelmed by the immensity of it all. Somehow she'd vaguely pictured San Jose as a sleepy village, but it was a big, bustling, terrifying *city*. They could never find Brian with this aimless wandering.

Finally they went to Bax's house. It was located in a pleasant residential neighborhood. The house itself was modest, but the yard was large and neatly cared for. Not by Bax, Reva suspected, unless he'd changed considerably. Somehow she doubted that he had.

Mikki opened the front door as soon as Drake parked the car at the curb. In spite of the tense, frightening situation, Reva couldn't escape a brief curiosity about the woman. She had bright red hair and an attractive, if rather full figure. She was also, Reva realized in surprise, several years older than Bax. The two women looked at each other awkwardly for a moment and then Mikki said she had coffee ready, and Reva nodded.

Over coffee, Mikki went a little further into the details of Brian's disappearance. He had been gone quite a while before they realized he was missing, because Mikki had thought he was with Bax. Some corner of Reva's mind noted a box, with a picture of a ball on it, sitting on the kitchen counter.

Mikki's mouth twisted slightly. "The soccer ball Bax has been promising Brian. He finally bought it yesterday—after Brian was gone. That's Bax, you know. Always a little late." Her voice was tight.

"He finally failed Brian once too often, didn't he?" Reva bit her lip, remembering Brian's disappointment over the promised baseball game.

Bax and his extravagant promises and bright plans, and every one of them empty and meaningless. That was the way Bax had always been. He'd let her down so many times, and now he was doing it to Brian.

"I think he means what he says at the time he says it," Mikki protested, but the defense sounded half-hearted and her voice trailed off. She sighed. "The sailing trip was never anything definite, just something one of Bax's friends said they might do. But Bax made it into a big deal for Brian, of course, and then . . ."

"And then Bax shrugged his shoulders and went off to drink beer with his buddies." It was all too familiar.

Mikki pressed her lips together and blinked several times in quick succession, as if to hold back tears, and Reva had the sudden suspicion that Brian wasn't the only one Bax had failed recently. Well, she hadn't come here to criticize Bax or to interfere in his marriage. She swallowed and forced herself to ask brisk questions, trying to figure out where Brian might have gone.

Mikki shook her head helplessly. "I've talked to all his friends, and he hadn't said anything to any of them about running away. My own first thought was that he'd probably decided to go home to you and Mark. He thinks a lot of you," she added, looking at Drake.

Drake had remained silent throughout the discussion, and now Reva realized that in her agitation she had forgotten the normal courtesy of introductions.

"This is my . . . friend, Drake McQuaid," she said awkwardly. "We flew down in his plane." She didn't elaborate on the subject of Mark.

"Oh, I see," Mikki said, though it was obvious she was a bit uncertain about the relationship between Reva and Drake.

The phone rang and Mikki went to answer it. "My brother," she explained when she returned. "Bax works for him in his insurance office. He was wondering if we'd heard anything about Brian."

Irrelevantly, Reva realized this explained Bax's job in insurance. She'd always wondered, with his irregular work history, how he'd managed to get the good job.

The three of them discussed the situation a little longer, and Reva thought Mikki could very well be right about Brian wanting to head home for Razor Bay. But how? He'd seen hitchhikers, of course. Reva's heart sank as she thought of innocent little Brian trying that, and the human vultures who might have gobbled him up. Or there was the bus. Was it possible an eight-year-old could get from one state to another alone? It seemed an unlikely thought, but on the scant possibility that it could be true, she tried to call Mark to ask if Brian had turned up in Razor Bay. No answer. The phone rang monotonously in what was obviously an empty house.

Reva and Drake scoured the highways leading out of town. They asked questions at the bus depot. They talked to city bus drivers, thinking Brian might not know the difference between local and interstate systems. They went to parks and poked fearfully around a seedy-looking warehouse district. Reva tried to call Mark again. Still no answer.

The search was utterly and totally fruitless. Brian might have been whisked off the face of the earth, for all anyone knew of him. Weary and defeated, they went back to Bax and Mikki's house when darkness forced the search to a halt.

Bax met them at the door. He looked hollow-eyed and exhausted, but there was a jumpy wariness about the way he ran his fingers through his hair, as if he half expected Reva to leap on him in a savage fury. As she was tempted to do, she thought grimly when Bax muttered something about not knowing "what got into that kid." Mikki had prepared a stew that could be kept hot and served any time, but Reva shook her head when Mikki offered the food. Her throat felt tight and closed, and her stomach was churning.

"You're welcome to stay here tonight," Mikki offered tentatively, without consulting her husband. "There's the bed in Brian's room . . . And I could make up the sofa," she added, evidently still uncertain of the relationship between Reva and Drake and not knowing whether to offer one bed or two.

"Thanks, but we'll stay at a motel," Reva said. "I'll call and tell you where we are so you can contact me if there's any word."

Reva's shoulders were sagging, and Drake braced her with a steady supporting arm as they made their way out to the car. She had the sinking feeling that Brian was slipping away from her, silently drifting farther and farther away into a gray fog where she could never find him. A newly

horrifying thought suddenly occurred to her. What if Brian
had tried to call her before he ran away? She hadn't been
there because she was off cavorting with Drake, having fun
and teasing and acting silly, as carefree as any schoolgirl
without responsibilities. What if Brian felt that in her absence she had failed him as miserably as his father had?

She started shivering and couldn't seem to stop. Oh,
Lord, she was as much at fault as Bax. If anything happened
to Brian . . . The thought was a chasm, a blankness, a darkness blotting out any future.

Drake stopped the car beside the plate-glass window of
a motel office and put his arms around her. He murmured
assurances, soothing her more with his voice than his words,
and finally Reva drew a shuddering breath. She had to get
control of herself. She couldn't help Brian if she fell to
pieces.

"You wait here," Drake murmured. "I'll get a room for
us."

Reva straightened, as if an electric shock had gone through
her. "No! I—I want a room by myself."

Drake paused, the car door half open. He looked at her
as if he thought he must have heard her incorrectly. *"What?"*

"I mean it," she said doggedly. "I can't—I *won't* be
making love while Brian might be lost or hurt or dead."

"Reva, I didn't have in mind that we'd rush to a room
and start tearing each other's clothes off." He sounded almost angry. "I just want to hold and comfort you."

"No!" she repeated wildly, almost panicking. She felt a
flood of hot shame and remorse. Her craving for Drake was
what had helped cause all this! If she had been available
when Brian needed her, perhaps none of this would have
happened.

Drake patted her arm soothingly. "Okay, okay. I'll get
two rooms. Now will you be all right for a minute while I
go make the arrangements?"

Reva nodded. He went inside and returned a few minutes
later with keys to rooms next to each other. He carried her
bag into one of them. Reva saw the television set and rushed
to turn it on, half expecting to hear some grisly story of the

discovery of an unidentified child's body.

She stared almost in disbelief at the football game on one channel, situation comedy on another. It all looked so normal—and her whole world was crumbling. She nodded numbly when Drake told her to relax in a hot bath.

"But before I go..." He tilted her chin up and forced her to look into his eyes. "Reva, you don't really think I'm so insensitive that all I have on my mind tonight is sex, do you? I know what you're going through."

"You can't know. You don't have a child of your own."

He flinched as if she'd struck him, but she didn't take back the cruel words. They were true. He couldn't know how she really felt. "I can sympathize," he told her.

Suddenly she wilted. She wanted desperately to lean against his strength, to bury herself in the warm shelter of his arms. Momentarily she let her forehead rest on the secure wall of his chest.

But she couldn't give in to the luxury of staying with him tonight.

She had a strange, almost mystical feeling that all this was somehow the result of her frivolous behavior this summer. Brian's disappearance was her punishment for being flighty and irresponsible, for going her merry way and putting Drake and the loving and excitement that went with him ahead of her real duties. And if she slept with Drake tonight, the punishment might go even further, to the reality of the unspeakable horrors that hovered on the the dark edges of her mind.

She jerked back from the contact with him. His face momentarily hardened, then he swallowed and touched his lips gently to her forehead.

"I'll bring you something to eat a little later."

She took a bath, keeping the phone on the floor beside the tub. It remained stubbornly, cruelly silent. Drake brought ham and cheese sandwiches, salad, and coffee, but Reva managed to swallow no more than a few choking bites. She waited until he was out of the room before removing her robe and slipping into the cold bed.

She was functioning on a strange plane of existence,

neither totally awake nor completely asleep as the bleak
night inched onward. Bizarre thoughts and dreams plowed
relentlessly through her mind, interspersed with agonies of
guilt and self-recrimination. A shrill noise was in a dream . . . a
horn honking as it bore down on a helpless, vulnerable
Brian . . . no, it was Brian himself screaming . . . Reva sat
bolt-upright in bed, heart thundering, body wet with a cold
perspiration. It took her a moment to realize the shrill sound
was the phone. She fumbled the instrument to her mouth
and ear.

"Yes?"

"Reva? This is Mikki. Brian is here. The police just
brought him. He's all right."

Oh, Lord, thank you, thank you, Reva breathed in silent,
eye-clenched relief. In a dozen efficient words, Mikki managed to convey everything Reva was desperate to hear.
Somehow she managed to mumble her gratitude.

"Would you like to come over now?" Mikki asked. Mikki
went on to say that Brian was already in bed, exhausted and
sound asleep, but Reva was welcome to come see him or
stay with him. Reva longed to see her son, but she knew
disturbing him in the middle of the night was hardly what
he needed now. She said she'd be at the house first thing
in the morning.

Hastily she wrapped a robe around her nightie and slipped
outside to tap on the next door. Drake was there instantly,
peering through the crack and then removing the chain when
he saw who it was.

"The police brought him home. He's okay."

He drew her into his arms and held her close. "I'm glad,"
he said simply. He smoothed her hair with a gentle brush
of his hand. She drew a shaky, shuddering breath of relief.
The nightmare of punishment was over.

Finally, when she started shivering, this time from actual
cold, he pulled her inside. She resisted momentarily, then
went with him, succumbing to the need for his strength and
comfort. They slept as a single unit in the center of the bed,
their bodies automatically fitting and melding together again
as they shifted position in sleep.

When Reva woke, she felt a momentary disorientation in the strange room. She was alone in the bed—was last night's phone call just a dream?

No. There was Drake, a smile on his face and a heavenly smelling cup of coffee in his hand.

"There are rolls and juice too. I knew you wouldn't take time for a restaurant meal before seeing Brian, so I went out to get something."

"Oh, Drake, thank you!" Impulsively she reached up and kissed him on the cheek when he handed her the coffee. "I don't know what I'd have done without you."

He smiled. "Hold that thought."

They ate quickly. Reva went back to her room and dressed. It was barely seven o'clock when they drove through the quiet residential streets to Bax's house.

"Just one question before we get there," Drake said, giving her a tentative sideways glance. "You were so positive about turning down Mikki's invitation to stay at the house last night. Did you have uneasy feelings about staying in a house where Bax was sleeping with another woman? Or didn't you want to sleep with *me* under the same roof with Bax?" He hesitated slightly. "He's a good-looking guy."

"The only reason I didn't want to stay in the same house with Bax was because I was afraid I'd try to throttle him if I was around him very long," Reva said fervently. She had long ago lost any interest in Bax's boyish good looks. The broken promises to *her* she had also been able to relegate to the unimportant past; the broken promises to Brian were something different.

"Okay." He smiled lightly. "I was just wondering. It kind of shook me when you insisted on two rooms last night. But I know how upset you were."

His smile and voice were understanding, showing her he bore her no grudge for briefly shutting him out. He obviously considered it a closed incident.

Yet it wasn't closed, Reva thought, momentarily troubled enough to hesitate before opening the car door when Drake stopped in front of Bax's house. In the light of day, she no longer had the sick feeling that Brian's disappearance was

some awful punishment for her sins. But she had been living
in something of a fantasy world these last weeks, enjoying
a shimmering golden bubble of unreality with Drake. Now
the bubble had burst. She was a *mother,* not some giddy
butterfly with nothing to do but flit blithely from here to
there, sampling fun and sex and excitement as if they were
some sweet nectar. If Brian had tried to call her before
running away, she must certainly accept a share of the responsibility for what could have been a tragedy.

Brian was still asleep and they all agreed he shouldn't
be wakened, though Reva did peek in on him to see with
her own eyes that he was whole and healthy. Over coffee
with Mikki, Reva learned that the police had found Brian
at the bus depot. He had indeed been trying to find a way
home. When Bax came out of the bathroom, Reva wasted
no time telling him that she was taking Brian home. He
blustered some objections but finally muttered that it was
all right with him. He'd come up to Oregon and spend a
weekend taking Brian hunting this fall.

He'd never change, Reva sighed to herself, knowing this
was another idea that would never materialize into fact.
When he left for work, he took Mikki's car because he had
neglected to get a new battery for his own, and they exchanged some veiled but decidedly acid remarks on that
subject.

Later Brian wandered out, rumpled, sleepy, and sweet-
faced.

"Mom!" he cried when he saw Reva. He hurled himself
at her without a trace of the grown-up reserve he sometimes
tried to assume. They hugged and kissed and chattered and
hugged some more. It was then that Reva learned for certain
he had tried to call her to tell her he wanted to come home.
When he couldn't get hold of either her or Mark, he ran
away.

Through all the joyful, tear-marked reunion, Drake remained in the background. When Reva finally remembered
to introduce Brian and Drake, Brian treated him politely but
formally, as he might some unfamiliar figure of authority.
After Brian had breakfast, they gathered up his things. Mikki

promised to send anything that was forgotten. Reva had the regretful feeling that Bax's marriage to Mikki wouldn't survive long.

On the drive to the airport, Brian clutched his new soccer ball and chattered eagerly about showing it to Mark. He was impressed with the plane but wanted to know why Mark hadn't come along on the flight.

The frequency with which Brian mentioned Mark did, in fact, make for a certain awkwardness on the trip home. Drake said nothing, nor did his expression give anything away, but by now Reva knew him well enough to sense a certain tension in him. For her, Brian's innocent chatter was a stunning reminder of just how closely attached Brian was to Mark. And right now she knew Brian desperately needed Mark's solid dependability. When Bax's marriage broke up—and there was no doubt in Reva's mind that it was only a question of *when,* not *if*—Bax would be no more than a phantom father, unavailable to Brian. Bax would be off on his merry way, thinking only of himself—just as he had done this summer.

Back in Razor Bay, Drake saw them safely to the house and then had to fly on to Portland immediately. Brian and Drake shook hands, and Brian thanked him for flying them home. It was sweet and a little comical to see Brian playing man of the house. Drake's mouth held a giveaway twitch of amusement, but he accepted the thanks gravely. Reva was proud of Brian, yet at the same time uncomfortably aware that he would have acted much differently with Mark. The first thing he did after Drake left, in fact, was try to call Mark. Again there was no answer, and Reva promised they'd check tomorrow to see if Mark had gone out of town.

Reva stayed away from the store the following day, wanting to spend the time with Brian. Drake called that evening, and she assured him that both she and Brian were fine. She learned from a neighbor that Mark had gone back up to Seattle for a few days. Brian quickly made contact with his old friends and, by the end of the week, life was, at least on the surface, back to normal. It was good to have Brian home again, and the house was busy with his chatter, ac- tivities, and friends.

Within herself, however, Reva was in turmoil, torn by conflicts of desire and duty, besieged by guilt and self- accusation. She felt alternating, conflicting, and sometimes wholly unreasonable anger with Drake, Mark, and herself. Uneasily she noted in Brian a small tendency to doubt things people told him, evidently a holdover from his experiences with Bax's unreliability. He belligerently demanded a *prom- ise* that a small friend wouldn't change his mind when the friend invited Brian to stay overnight Saturday night. He kept complaining about Mark's absence, as if he were be- ginning to doubt him, too.

When Saturday night came, Brian had a small conflict of his own. He wanted to spend the night with his friend, but he seemed suspicious that Reva might disappear into thin air if he went away for a night. Evidently that time of crisis when he'd tried to call and been unable to reach her had had a lasting impression on him. He finally, however, went a bit reluctantly to the friend's house, and Reva was relieved. She needed a little time alone.

She turned to her usual method of regaining tranquility, an evening walk alone on the beach, hoping the timeless quality of wind and waves would do something to soothe the unrest within her.

Unhappily, her turmoil all boiled down to one brutal point. She had made a fool of herself this summer, playing around with Drake, making love recklessly as if she were some footloose single instead of a responsible mother. She must call a halt to the foolishness. It was not, after all, undying love between Reva and Drake; it was sex. Granted, it was terrific sex, fantastic sex, everything sex could and should be—playful, loving, joyous, sharing, passionate. But just sex, nonetheless.

As Mark had once said, it surely wasn't important enough to throw away the relationship with him and their children. Brian needed Mark as a father, just as Jade needed Reva for a mother. She and Mark had that mutual interest in their children going for them, plus a mutual respect—though that had been temporarily damaged by her fling with Drake, of course. They seldom argued. Perhaps they even loved each other . . . in a way.

What she felt for Mark wasn't what she had always thought—hoped—love was. Yet her notion of love was probably idealistic, unrealistic, and over-romanticized. She must be practical and keep her feet firmly on the ground and think of what was best for Brian.

Grow up, Reva Jonathan, she admonished herself. Stop acting like some innocent adolescent, all starry-eyed about romance and love.

At the far end of the sandy beach, where a massive ledge of jagged rock barricaded the way, she turned and started back along the curving crescent of sand.

Then she saw him, just a dark figure far up the beach, but familiar—so achingly familiar. He waved and, after a moment's hesitation, she waved back. She felt strangely weak-kneed at the sight of him. He broke into a jog, dark hair falling carelessly across his forehead, feet leaving imprints in the damp sand. One part of her longed to break free and run joyously to meet him, but she held herself back, resolutely denying the flood of eagerness within her.

He jogged up to her, flashing that irresistible smile. He was so damnably handsome, so unabashedly virile, so exciting in his mere presence. She was suddenly angry with his physical attributes and her own female reaction to his sexual attractiveness.

"Wow, when you said you sometimes took a little walk on the beach in the evening, you really meant it, didn't you?" he commented, eyeing the distance she had traversed. He planted a slightly breathless kiss on her mouth.

She drew back. "How did you know I was here?"

"Your neighbor saw you leave and told me you'd probably come down here." He linked his hand with hers and thrust both in his deep pocket. By now the rising evening breeze had a bite to it. "How's everything going?"

"Fine."

"Brian settling back to normal?" he asked. Reva nodded.

He hesitated and then asked, "Did he get hold of Mark?"

"Mark is still out of town."

"Where's Brian tonight?"

"Staying overnight with a friend." She knew what Drake was thinking when she revealed that bit of information, of course. He was planning to spend the night with her.

For a moment, temptation almost overcame her resolve. One more night of magic in his arms, a few last moments of wild and passionate lovemaking . . .

No. She'd made up her mind.

"My son is a fact of life, Drake. He's my responsibility."

"Did I say he wasn't?" Drake countered. He looked a little puzzled by her argumentative tone of voice. "In fact, I guess I have a little unasked-for advice to give about him."

She eyed him warily. What did he know of children? "Such as?"

"You've just been through a terrifying experience with Brian. It was frightening for him, too. But you have to remember that Brian is a very bright boy, and he's going to figure out that running away *worked*."

"What do you mean 'worked'?" Reva demanded sharply. They moved up the beach as the incoming tide washed a surge of foam toward their feet. "You sound as if he planned it."

"No, I don't mean that. But from Brian's point of view, what he did was very effective. It brought attention and immediate and positive reaction. It brought *you* running. It got him home instantly, without arguments. It even made his father live up to his promise about the soccer ball. All I'm saying is that Brian is bright enough to figure out that, if it worked once, it might work again. Kids aren't above playing on their parents' guilty consciences."

Some corner of Reva's mind acknowledged that Drake could be right, but the small thought was lost in a rush of protectiveness toward her son. Brian could have been killed wandering alone in that big city! "Are you saying I shouldn't have gone to him?" she said in a challenging tone.

"No, of course not."

"I don't see that you're in any position to give advice

about child-raising," Reva said frigidly. "You don't have—"

"Any children," he finished. "I knew you were going to say that. And it's true, of course. I'm a little short on experience in raising kids. But there's nothing wrong with my memory of my own childhood, and I can very well remember my own none-too-admirable but very effective manipulation of my parents during and after their divorce. I knew exactly how to play them off against each other to get what I wanted. For a while I was a ten-year-old despot."

Reva glanced up at him, surprised at the somewhat rueful admission of his own past misdeeds. "So what happened?" she asked with reluctant curiosity.

"They finally figured out what I was doing and got together enough to present me with a united front—and the laying down of a few mutually enforced rules."

Something she and Bax would never be able to do, Reva knew. She also had to admit, in spite of her defensive feeling toward Brian, that he occasionally did need a strong hand to guide him. Strong but loving. And most of all he needed the reliable dependability his real father could never provide him.

And that was exactly what she intended to give him.

"I'm just saying, given Brian's father's unreliability, that you're the one who will have to—"

"Brian will have the kind of solid, dependable father he needs." Reva lifted her head, letting the wind whip through her hair. She knew the reaction her next announcement was going to bring. "I've decided to marry Mark."

*"What?"* Drake stopped dead still, yanking her to a halt with him. "When did you decide this?"

"Over a . . . period of time."

"And have you given Mark the good news yet?" he asked sardonically. He faced her, his expression harsh and raw against the background of crashing seas and wave-washed rocks. "Don't you think there's the slight possibility that he might feel differently about marriage when he knows about us?"

"He already knows about us. He said he was willing to

take me back when I came to my senses."

"How noble of him," Drake said mockingly. "And do you call deciding to marry a man you don't love 'coming to your senses'?" He paused, eyes narrowing. "Or maybe this is just a pressure tactic you're using on *me*."

"Pressure tactic on you! What do you mean by that?"

But Reva knew what he meant. He was suggesting she was trying to pressure *him* into marriage! Fury blazed through her at the accusation, a hot tide that raged like the waves boiling around jagged offshore rocks. She jerked her hand from his pocket and stalked up the beach, her back held rigid with anger.

She had gone no more than a dozen strides before he yanked her to a halt again. His dark eyes bored into hers. His mouth had a hard twist.

"You don't have to use pressure, Reva," he said, scowling. "I want to marry you."

"Why, how generous of you," she mocked. "How noble of you! But no thanks!"

"Look, I'm sorry about what I said just now. It was uncalled for. But you know you can be infuriatingly stubborn and exasperating. Let's go up to the house and talk this over."

"There's nothing to talk over. I've decided to marry Mark."

"Why? You don't love him. You couldn't love him and make love with me the way you do." His voice held the depth of conviction.

"Love doesn't have to be so...physical," Reva said evasively. She realized that in their anger and agitation, the surging water had washed unnoticed around their feet. Oddly, she couldn't seem to feel the wetness, even though her shoes were soaked. She felt strangely numb.

"You're marrying him solely to give Brian a father, aren't you?" Drake pushed her away from the attacking water, toward a scattering of driftwood logs. "Reva, I realize I haven't the experience Mark has at being a father, or his close relationship with Brian, and I can't offer you a ready-made daughter, but—"

"But you can offer me a good time in bed."

Drake winced at her blunt words. "You don't waste time beating around the bush, do you?" he muttered.

They sat on a driftwood log, sheltered a little from the wind by the tentacled arc of the log's roots spreading upward. She shook her head helplessly, her anger softened by his wry comment.

"Drake, we've had fun. I've loved every minute of it. Even the battling with you has been exhilarating. I appreciate your flying me to San Jose and helping search for Brian. But I'm a mother, and you're just not the husbandly, fatherly type."

"Why not?" he demanded.

"Oh, Drake . . ." She shook her head, smiling through a sudden shimmer of tears. "You're too handsome, too sexy, too macho, too virile. You have too much dash and fire. You're too adventurous, too flashy, too willing to take chances. You generate sparks and excitement. Maybe you said it all the time you said you doubted you were the type of man a girl brought home to mother."

"Somehow I never thought of myself as *flashy*," he murmured, picking out the one word to protest. "Maybe it's the mustache." He fingered the rakish twist of hair above his lip, a remnant of the familiar dance of wicked amusement in his eyes. "I could always shave it off, you know."

"You're not taking me seriously!" she protested angrily.

"You can't *be* serious," he shot back. "Reva, I'm sure the man is a good, decent guy. He'll make some dependent, pliable woman a wonderful husband. But that isn't you! He bores you. Admit it! He disapproves of your career with the store. Your children are all you have in common. And I will not accept your judgment that I wouldn't make a good husband or father just because I don't look the part."

"Oh, Drake, it isn't just your mustache or looks." She sighed and shook her head again. "Look at your life. You live in an adults-only apartment complex without the presence or interference of children. You were appalled at Matt Wyland's domestic life. You're accustomed to coming and going as you please, flying off to new adventures on a whim of the moment. You can't do that when you have the responsibility of a child, and I have that responsibility. You can't make love in the moonlight on the living-room floor when a child is apt to come stumbling through the room. And I remember you once saying you were glad you didn't have any children of your own," she added suddenly.

"Reva, you're twisting things. Just because I was glad Gale and I didn't have children doesn't mean I'm unalterably opposed to them!" An edge of frustrated anger had returned to his voice.

He stared, frowning, across the lash of waves. The last rays of the sinking sun cut a golden path across the rolling surface of silver-blue water. It gave a strange illusion of solidity, as if one could walk to the edge of the world on that glittering streak.

Drake straightened his shoulders and began again. He smiled a little ruefully. "This is a new problem for me, you know. I'm not usually in the position of trying to prove what a great husband and father I'd make." His voice held tight humor. "More often I'm trying to escape the clutches of some woman who is all too eager to trap me into marriage and fatherhood."

"The problems of being a sex symbol," Reva murmured unsympathetically.

"Look, I know I haven't spent the last few years living like the typical suburban husband coping with crabgrass and Little League, but I'm not some playboy with no sense of responsibility."

"Brian needs Mark," Reva reiterated doggedly, ignoring his arguments.

"What do *you* need?" he challenged.

"My needs don't count!"

"Don't they? Tell me that a year from now when you're trapped in a loveless marriage. Tell me that a dozen years from now, when your children are grown and gone, and all you and Mark have is the emptiness of each other." His voice and look scorched her with contempt as he stood up, dark hair battered by the wind. "In the meantime, congratulations. You certainly win the award for Mother Making the Most Noble Sacrifice of the Year."

"Marrying Mark isn't a sacrifice!"

Drake's brilliant flash of smile was as taunting as the words that followed. "Isn't it?"

# Chapter Nine

SHE WATCHED HIM GO, feeling as if a vein had been opened and the life and strength were flowing out of her, following his angry strides across the sand. She couldn't simply let him stalk out of her life, taking some vital core of her being with him! One last night in his arms, she thought, giving in to the whirlpool pull of temptation. Just one more...

"Drake!" she screamed. "Drake!"

But her frantic scream was whipped away by the wind, lost among the shrieking gulls and scudding clouds. She ran after him, but by now the wind had risen until each stride was a battle against some unseen force that took fiendish glee in holding her back. He never once looked back at her. By the time she reached the house, breathless, her side aching, there was no sign he had ever been there.

She felt a sudden rage of fury with the wind, with the limits of time, and cruelties of fate. All she wanted was one more night with him. One! Couldn't she have been allowed just that much?

Then her fury sagged, defeated by honesty. One more night with Drake would never be enough. Given one more night, she'd simply crave another, and another.

Yes, it was better this way, she thought dully. She left

a trail of damp, sandy tracks as she clumped inside the house. She had made up her mind and there was no point torturing herself with "just once more," like some desperate alcoholic snatching that one last drink before going on the wagon and then finding the addiction could not be broken.

She had to put Drake out of her mind and heart, remove his imprint from her emotions and body, break the addiction that threatened to sabotage her good intentions and responsibilities. She reminded herself again that sex, not love, was the basic attraction between them.

Wasn't it? And where was the dividing line?

With a kind of frantic desperation she ran to the phone and dialed Mark's number. She let the phone ring and ring, but there was no answer. Oh, damn, damn, damn, she thought with a groan. Why wasn't he there when she needed him? Why didn't he come home so she could tell him that she was going to marry him before she did something irreparably wild and foolish? Once she had made a positive commitment to him, her basic principles of loyalty and honesty, her standards of right and wrong, would surely hold her steady to the course she had chosen.

On sudden inspiration she fumbled in the drawer by the phone and came up with the scrap of paper on which Mark had written the number where he could be reached on his previous trip to Seattle. With shaky hands she dialed, got a maternal-sounding older woman who was evidently Jade's grandmother, and finally Mark was on the line.

"Is anything wrong?" he asked sharply when he recognized Reva's voice.

She explained briefly about Brian's disappearance and added that everything was fine now, except that Brian was anxious to see him. "I'm anxious to see you too," she added awkwardly. "Will you be coming home soon?"

"We're planning to stay until next weekend. Jade is taking trampoline lessons that won't be finished until then."

"Oh." Reva hesitated, then forged ahead. "Mark, I'd really like to talk to you *soon*. As soon as possible. About . . . us."

"I see." Mark's voice held guarded interest. "The situation has changed?"

"Perhaps I've . . . come to my senses."

"Good." His tone held a brisk satisfaction, as if he'd always known she'd see the error of her frivolous ways. "If we could discuss it on the phone?"

"I'd really prefer to talk to you in person."

There were some muffled sounds as Mark evidently consulted with Jade. "We'll leave here Friday, stay with some friends in Portland Friday night, and get home Saturday."

"Not until next Saturday?" Reva repeated, dismayed. She needed to get this settled *now!* "Couldn't you come home earlier and then go back and get Jade?"

"That would mean an extra trip."

"Yes, of course." Reva stifled a sigh. Mark would never let romance overrule practicality. "Next Saturday then. I'll have dinner ready about six." Mark liked to eat fairly early. "For just the two of us," she added, to emphasize the intimate nature of the talk.

"Fine. I'll be there."

Reva fought an unruly surge of annoyance as she put down the phone. Mark obviously knew what she intended. Was this delaying tactic his way of punishing her? Probably not, she decided, sighing. Mark was simply being Mark—practical, logical. He wouldn't impulsively shorten the planned length of his stay for anything less than a life-or-death emergency. He had no doubt looked ahead, decided they'd have a lifetime together, and concluded that a week's delay now was unimportant. His practical nature, solid dependability, and lack of frivolous impulsiveness were among the traits for which she had chosen to marry him, of course, so she shouldn't complain about those characteristics now. She should simply remember that he had said he'd be at the house Saturday night, and that meant he'd be there.

Yet if just this *once* he could have thrown prudent judgment to the winds and raced recklessly to claim her immediately . . .

She sighed again. She would just have to learn to be

more patient. Patience was another of the virtues Mark both possessed and admired.

The week dragged along. Brian, as before the visit to his father, spent his days under the watchful eye of a dependable neighbor. Workmen swarmed around the building now, but business at Cheese 'n' Stuff was reasonably good. The work drew as many interested onlookers to the building as it drove away. Reva begged a couple of the old claw-footed bathtubs and used them to hold an interesting display of sale crackers. Through the newspaper and local historical society she rounded up and displayed some old clippings and photographs about the building and its varied uses over the years, including a brief, shady period as a house of burlesque. She advertised a special sale to announce her new policy of staying open late on Friday evenings.

She made careful plans for the Saturday-night dinner with Mark. She considered chicken Kiev for the meal but decided against it and chose old reliable fried chicken instead, plus mashed potatoes and gravy, green salad, and chocolate cake. The good, solid, all-American type of meal Mark liked. She would acknowledge to him that he was right: their relationship was far more important than a tawdry affair. He would forgive her magnanimously. Everything would be just as it used to be before Drake McQuaid tore through her life like a tornado whirling through a bowl of feathers.

She made a determined effort to close her mind to thoughts of Drake, to wall off memories of the excitement, fun, and rapturous lovemaking she had known with him. But there were cracks in the wall, and memories leaked out. And they were insidious memories, not only of lovemaking that soared to undreamed-of heights, but also of tenderness and teasing, laughing and fighting, easy chatter and comfortable silence.

She had the sinking feeling that nothing could ever again be the same as it was before Drake catapulted into her life.

Correct, she told herself with a hard mental shake. The situation *was* changed; it was much better now. She had her priorities straight. The fling with Drake had nudged her into a real commitment with Mark.

Not yet a *real* commitment, some small, sly voice within her reminded. Not until Saturday night when she said the words would it be a real commitment.

She quickly buried the treacherous thought. Drake was out of her life.

The Friday-night sale was a surprising success. An unusually balmly evening helped bring people strolling downtown. Reva and Beth moved some of the non-refrigerated items outside for people to paw through. The small packages of cheese and crackers they had made up with "Eat Me Now" labels sold quite nicely, but Reva realized quickly that she should also have soft drinks to offer.

A little before nine o'clock, Beth helped carry things back inside, then left with her boyfriend. Reva started to close up. She covered the refrigerated display cases and straightened the pyramid of exotic teas someone had knocked awry. She was at the door, ready to lock it, when a strength greater than her own thrust the door open.

"Drake!" She had wondered what would happen when she faced a moment such as this, and now she felt hot and cold jitters, as if her nerves had short-circuited. He was wearing jeans and a black turtleneck shirt that clung to his muscular chest and broad shoulders. His eyes had the reckless diamond glitter of someone operating on a dare. He exuded a male-animal vigor and vitality and that quality of dangerous verve that always gave her a shivery tingle.

"Wh—what are you doing here?"

"I just flew in on a whim of the moment." He repeated the words, which she had once used against him, with diabolical mockery.

"On business?"

"If I wanted to see my construction superintendent, I imagine I'd have come during working hours, don't you?" he said tauntingly, with a smile that matched the glitter of his eyes. He glanced around. "Where's your beloved betrothed?" He reached for her hand and trapped it before she could snatch it say. "What, no ring yet? Ah, but I forgot. Mark probably wouldn't waste time or money on glittery little baubles. Too impractical. Too flashy."

"Have you been drinking?" Reva demanded suspiciously.

He dropped her hand, dropping with it the brilliantly humorless smile. The expression that remained was dark granite. "No, I have not been drinking. If I thought going on a weekend drunk would make me forget you, I'd be tempted to do it. But it wouldn't work. You'd still be there, along with the hangover, when I sobered up." He sounded uncharacteristically bitter.

"What do you want? Why did you come here?"

Drake shrugged. Reva tried not to let her eyes follow the play of muscles beneath the form-fitting shirt.

"Maybe I wanted to buy cheese from my favorite store." He opened a display case, snatched up a wrapped package without looking at it, and flung it on the counter like a challenge.

Reva met the challenge. "The store is closed."

"Good." His smile returned to lethal brilliance. "Then we can talk."

"No."

"Yes."

Reva hesitated, lower lip caught nervously between her teeth. He obviously would not leave, yet they couldn't just stand here in the middle of the store arguing into the small hours of the night. If she went home, she had the feeling he'd follow relentlessly. And the house was empty, because Brian was staying overnight at the sitter's. She dare not risk the temptation of being too intimately alone with Drake. She hadn't that much confidence in her will power.

"Very well. We can talk for a minute in the back room."

She kept her head high as she finished the closing-up routine. She dimmed the lights, and he held the door to the back room open. She was careful not to touch him as she swept past him into the cluttered room. She walked briskly to her old oak desk and snapped on the lamp. The stained-glass shade threw a soft rainbow of light that was all too suggestively intimate. Quickly she yanked the string controlling the bare bulb overhead, which served only to bring the daybed into glaring focus. Flustered, Reva whirled to face him, her body half shielded by the swivel chair at the desk.

"I'm very busy, so—"

"Everything is settled with Mark?" Drake cut in without polite preliminaries.

"Not yet," she answered reluctantly.

He lifted a dark eyebrow. "You're having second thoughts?"

"No! Mark will be back from Seattle tomorrow. We have a date for dinner at my house. I'll tell him then. But I'm sure he already knows why I want to see him."

"And what will you tell him? That you're madly in love with him and just now realized it?" Drake asked derisively. He perched on the edge of the desk, one lean leg dangling lazily. Even the harsh glare of the bare bulb overhead failed to diminish the handsome lines of his face and dark flash of his eyes. "Or will you be honest and tell him you've decided to marry him for your son's sake, in spite of the fact that you're in love with another man?"

"I want . . . I'm not . . ." Reva choked over his arrogance. "How dare you come in here and brazenly claim I'm in love with you!"

"How dare you go into some city-council meeting and brazenly stop my mall project cold? How dare you sit on top of your shaky old ladder and coerce me into letting you stay in this building. We do it because we're two of a kind, Reva. We're stubborn and determined and willing to take chances. We go after what we want—and I want *you.*"

He slid along the desk until his head was above hers and she was forced to look up into his eyes. Deliberately he cupped his hands around her face and kissed her mouth. It was a deep, unhurried kiss, thorough and masterful. She knew she should pull away, but she was held by some magnetic force greater than her own will, a force that had nothing to do with physical strength. The kiss lifted her, evaporated her protective wall of coolness into a steamy haze of desire that was no protection at all. Her response was terrifyingly immediate and intense, her body instantly remembering the thrill of total fulfillment that followed Drake's deep, sensuous kisses.

The hot tendrils of yearning reached deep inside her, curling among vital organs and winding into the very core of her femininity. She would not let herself return the kiss, she vowed fiercely. She would not allow her tongue to meet the probing warmth of his, or her hands to creep into the crisp darkness of his hair...but neither could she force herself to jerk away and ruthlessly end the sweet torment. She could let the embrace go no further than this kiss, yet when he started to lift his head she held his mouth for one greedy moment longer.

"Reva..." He shook his head, his voice husky with a mixture of anger and desire. "I've spent all week going crazy thinking about you." His cupped hands tightened, and his smoldering gaze was on her mouth.

She clutched his wrists with her hand. "Drake...don't! Why have you come here? Why are you doing this to me—to *us?*" she begged distractedly. "Why can't you just accept—"

"Why can't you accept the fact that we belong together?" His hands moved around to tangle almost harshly in her hair. "Why can't you realize that marrying Mark would be the worst mistake of your life?"

"No! The mistake was in letting myself become involved with you!"

"Why?" he demanded. "Because now you know there's more to love than your lukewarm little relationship with Mark? Because now you know that you'll never be satisfied with the life the two of you will have together?"

"I will be satisfied!" she returned fiercely.

"Will you?"

He smiled faintly, mockingly. His hands slid down her throat, pausing leisurely to explore the throbbing pulse and massage the taut cords. His fingertips slipped lower to release the top button of her blouse.

"Don't..." she told him, breathing in deeply. But her hands, still clasped around his wrists, made no move to stop him. She stared into his eyes, lips parted, like some wild animal trapped in the mesmerizing beam of a spotlight.

He moved to the second button, then with slow deliberation to the third. She gritted her teeth in an agony of frustration with the slow-motion progress, longing to rip buttons and barriers aside. She felt her swelling breasts strain against the lacy bra that separated the sensitive, yearning peaks from the tender fire of his fingertips. He kissed the soft slope of skin above the lace.

"Will you never think of this?" he whispered. "Will you never remember the hours of love we shared?"

Yes, she thought wildly. She would remember. She would remember and long for his kisses and caresses. She would ache to run her hands over his smooth hard body, share his husky laughter, tease and delight him with inventive playfulness or demanding passion.

But she must not think of that, must not give into treacherous temptation. She had decided what must be done; she must not falter now! When he reached for the fastener on her bra, she ducked beneath his arms and scrambled away. She faced him from behind the protection of the swivel chair, her chest rising and falling as if she had been running. Her blouse was open, but the bra was still securely in place.

"Drake, you're just making this a hundred times more difficult. I've made up my mind! I *am* going to marry Mark."

"Because he's reliable. Dependable. Stable. Because he'll make a good father for Brian."

"Yes!"

"And what makes you so damn sure I wouldn't make a good father?"

"Brian acts differently toward you than he does toward Mark." She swiveled the chair as he took a sidestep to detour it, keeping it between them.

"Of course he does." Drake sounded exasperated. "We hardly know each other yet." Reluctantly he added, "And it is, I suppose, remotely possible that we wouldn't ever be as close as he and Mark are, but if we all tried—"

"I know I have to do what I think is best for my son,"

she said doggedly. She fumbled with the buttons of her blouse, trying to conceal the betrayal of nipples straining against white lace.

"Reva, it isn't *enough*. Can't you see that?" He started toward her again, and when she again tried to hide behind the chair, he flung it impatiently aside, skidding it to an angled tilt against the floor. He grabbed her upper arms and took a deep breath, struggling to control his anger against her unyielding attitude. "I can understand your need to provide your son with a steady, dependable father. It's something you have to consider in the man you marry. But you can't make it the only consideration. The man you marry has to be a mate for you as well as a father for your son. Is Mark that man? Will Mark let you be *you?*"

Reva didn't answer, and he pressed relentlessly onward.

"Brian is growing up, Reva. So is Mark's daughter. What will you have when they're grown and gone? What will you have for yourself in the years between now and then?"

"The satisfaction of knowing I did what was right!" Reva retorted defiantly.

"By marrying a man you don't love? Is that the way to raise your son?"

"People learn to love each other."

"Sometimes they also learn to hate each other," he shot back grimly.

She swallowed. "I like Mark. I respect him," she said carefully. "Mark and I are good friends."

"Perhaps you are," Drake agreed. His hands moved down to her waist, then lower to lock her body into intimate contact with his as he added softly. "But *we* are lovers."

Reva caught her breath. The whispered reminder echoed like a shout in the small, silent room.

"And where does that fit into your neat little scheme of things?" he asked with soft, deadly insistence.

"It's . . . irrelevant," she answered, but the words came out thick and fuzzy, caught in a conflict between mind and body. Because at this moment nothing on earth felt more relevant than the hard thrust of Drake's male form against her own taut body. His lips whispered kisses over her closed eyes and clenched lips, and she felt the hot wall of his chest through the opening of her still-unbuttoned blouse. His thighs were muscled iron against her legs, and his hands lifted her until her toes barely touched the floor, sliding her over the hard ridge of his male outlines. She felt a fiery surge of demand from her own body, a frenzy of need to possess and be possessed in the total union that made them a single living, loving force.

Yet when his weight shifted to lift her into his arms, she struggled against him. He was tricking her, some part of her mind warned through the haze of desire. He was using her own traitorous flesh against her. She got her hands against his shoulders and shoved. "You said when you barged in here that you wanted to talk," she told him, panting. "This isn't *talk!*"

"Communication doesn't necessarily have to be verbal," he argued softly. "You're telling me right now that you want me."

"No, I'm not! I don't—" But even as her mouth protested and her hands and arms shoved against him, her body arched to cling to his.

He reached down and clasped her by the straining curve of her buttocks, lifting her until her legs wound instinctively around him. He held her there, his palms cupped beneath her, and her hands crept around his neck.

"Drake, you can't do this." She shook her head in protest. "I've made up my mind."

"You've 'come to your senses.'" His voice was mocking even as his hands guided her into a tantalizing rocking motion against him.

"Yes!"

"Reva, I'm going to make love to you." His voice was still soft, huskily intimate, but there was no mistaking the deadly intent in it. "Here? Your house? My room at the inn?"

Reva unwrapped her legs from their locked position around his body, suddenly outraged by his calm audacity. She tried to slap his face, but all her wild swing succeeded in doing was catching the string attached to the bare bulb overhead.

The bulb flicked out, leaving the room in the warm tinted glow from the small stained-glass lamp on her desk.

"Here then," Drake said pleasantly. With one arm firmly clamped around her waist, he used the other to sweep empty boxes and cartons from the narrow bed.

Reva stood rigid, fighting the temptation to fling herself into a wild abandon of lovemaking with him. The room felt strangely different from its usual mundane daytime use as office and repository for supplies and miscellaneous. The clutter was lost in soft shadows, and there was an intimacy to the locked silence surrounding them. Now it was a clandestine love nest, hidden from the world. Or was it that Drake's presence made the room different, that anywhere with him was a setting for love?

"I'm leaving," Reva suddenly muttered thickly.

She whirled toward the door. He reached for her. She slithered out of his grasp, only to realize that freedom had come at the expense of her blouse. It hung from his clenched fist for a moment, and then he flung it to the far side of the bed. She felt a first small tremble of fear and apprehension. They were alone behind locked doors, and Drake McQuaid was neither predictable nor under the restraint of civilized convention. He made his own rules.

She crossed her hands defensively over her half-naked breasts, then dropped clenched fists to her sides, her breasts uplifted defiantly. "Is this what you do when a woman turns you down?" she demanded, summoning a protective barrier of scornful superiority. "Force her?"

"If I have to use force to ram some sense into her," he told her levelly.

He moved toward her, slowly but relentlessly. She clutched the doorknob behind her, her eyes scanning the room frantically. Surely there was a smock, jacket, something she could snatch to cover herself and run. She couldn't race out into the night half undressed!

"Keep . . . keep away from me," she warned.

"No. I told you I'm going to make love to you, and I keep my word." His voice was implacable but his smile was a lazy, wicked flash. "Isn't dependability one of the qualities you insist upon?"

She let go of the doorknob in time to make a protective barrier of her uplifted palms, her jaw clenched. But he assaulted the barrier with a surprise attack against which she had prepared no defense. He caught the uplifted hands in his and kissed each fingertip with a fiery tenderness, moving to her palms and then the curve of her wrists, where the racing pulse echoed the thunder of her heartbeat.

"Is this too much force?" he murmured as his mouth moved up her bare arm, unimpeded by resistance. He showered her shoulders with kisses and nibbled the soft lobe of her ear until small, delicious tingles rippled through her.

"Drake, this isn't fair . . ." she protested in a small moan, but it was a halfhearted protest at best. Under his deft touch the bra slipped unresistingly from her body.

Her breasts reacted as if just released from some unhappy restraining prison and gloried in the freedom. Already taut with arousal, they swelled to new peaks of sensitivity. He cupped them gently, dipping tender lips to each. Reva felt a swaying dizziness as the sweet, forbidden torment went on and on . . . gentle tongue flicks, tiny nips and tugs, tease of lips and squeeze of fingertips. She had promised herself she would not give in to this. She would not let him tempt her into the bottomless trap of his lovemaking.

She would not wrap her arms around his neck or let him sweep her into his arms and carry her to the bed . . . Yet even as she vowed it, she was looking up into the shadows of the ceiling, her head pillowed against his shoulder as he carried her with swift strides across the small room.

"Reva—"

Whatever he started to say didn't get finished. His foot caught on the overturned chair, and they both sprawled forward. He twisted, trying to keep from crushing her against the metal side of the bed. Something hit the wall with a thunderous thud.

"Drake! Drake, are you all right?" she cried, looking down into his closed eyes.

He shook his head to clear it. "I think so. But I'm beginning to think I should carry disaster insurance around you."

Now that she knew he was uninjured, Reva's momentary concern turned to outrage. "Well, it's your own fault. Practically trying to rape me, forcing me to—"

"This probably wouldn't be a really good time to yell about force and rape," he pointed out helpfully. "Not if you want to be believed."

She was sprawled over him, her body pinning his to the bed as if she were the aggressor trying to force him into submission. Her naked breasts were pressed against his chest, and he was the one with evidence of a blow to the head.

"Help," Drake cried in a small, unrecognizable yelp as he grinned up at her. "This woman is trying to—"

"You—you're impossible!" Reva said sputtering. "You'd probably tell some investigating officer that I locked you in here and leaped on you aflame with uncontrollable lust."

"Aflame with lust," he repeated solemnly. "I like that." He kissed her on the throat. "I can see the headlines now: "Lust-crazed cheese merchant forces landlord into acts of sexual depravity. See page ten for lurid details."

"Oh, Drake." Reva shook her head helplessly, laughing while her eyes filled with a shimmer of tears. "It's . . . impossible. Can't you see that? Anything more than *this* between us is impossible."

"No, I can't see that. All I see is that you and I are meant for each other." He pulled her head down and kissed her with a sweet, gentle tenderness.

But there isn't just you and me, Reva echoed silently, even as her senses reveled in the kiss. There's you and me and Brian—and my responsibility and duty to him.

"Reva, you know I'd never force you against your will, don't you?" he asked huskily, letting his head drop back to the bed. "I just want to love some sense into you. For a smart woman, you're making such a hell of a mistake!"

"If I were so smart, I wouldn't have gotten involved with you."

"We're back to that." He sounded both frustrated and

exasperated. He sighed. "Okay, maybe I'm a little thick-headed. Tell me again all the reasons you *are* going to marry Mark and *aren't* going to marry me. Lay them all out. Draw diagrams if you have to."

Reva shook her head. "I don't see—"

*"Tell me!"*

Reva rolled away from him on the bed, though it was too narrow to escape the contact of his warm body. She flung one hand over her eyes to shut out the distraction of his intent gaze and concentrate on dredging up all the good logic behind her decision. She talked of the worries she had about Brian, his insecurities and occasional retreats from people, his need for stability. She reiterated all the good qualities in Mark that had originally attracted her to him, those qualities that were so totally opposite Bax's careless-ness and irresponsibility, the same qualities that would make Mark a good father for Brian.

Drake made no comment, offered no argument. He did no more than rest his hand on the bare skin beneath her breasts and throw a possessive knee over her legs, but even those small points of contact made it difficult for Reva to keep her mind on unemotional reasoning and cold logic. His hand felt rough-warm, and the irrelevant thought kept sneaking into her mind that it would feel so good, so warm and protective, on her breast. But the hand didn't move, deliberately denying her the warm touch, and she twisted restlessly, her line of logic broken momentarily. She shiv-ered lightly.

"Cold?"

"I've complained to the landlord about the heating sys-tem," she retorted lightly, opening her eyes to look at him, "but he—"

"Never let it be said Century Development doesn't take care of its tenants." Drake lifted her and shifted his own weight until he managed to drag a blanket out from beneath them. He gathered Reva into his arms and wrapped the blanket around their entwined forms. "How's that for per-sonal attention from the landlord?"

She snuggled into his warmth in spite of warning flares

rocketing through her mind. "Will I be billed for extras?"

"You might. The price could be high," he warned.

"Such as?" She tilted her head back to look at him. His eyes had a dark, devilish gleam.

"Now let's see," he mused. "Just what sort of payment could I demand from a beautiful, sexy woman? I'm sure I'll think of *something . . .*" He lifted her thigh and wrapped her leg around his body. Then he sighed. "With my luck, however, she'll probably reward me with cheese."

"Not necessarily."

Reva lifted herself on one elbow and kissed him full on the mouth. The kiss was playfully exaggerated at first, her tongue aggressive in his mouth, her lips grinding against his and teeth clashing. Yet, like two healthy young animals in whom a playful scrap suddenly turns to fierce battle, the playfulness changed to a spurting flame of passion. He rolled over her, pinning her to the narrow bed with his weight and strength. Her legs wound around his, locking him against her as his mouth plundered her with a sweet, tender violence.

"I won't let you go," he murmured fiercely against her lips. "I won't let you escape."

But at this moment escape was the farthest thing from Reva's mind. She wanted only to burrow closer to him, to remove the frustrating barriers of fabric that separated the elemental warmth of his body from hers, to know again the total union with him . . .

She had crossed some invisible line and there was no turning back.

She slipped her hands beneath the clinging knit shirt and explored the long muscles of his back and rippled line of his spine. With a small growl of impatience he ripped the shirt away, and then nothing separated the sensitive swell of her breasts from his naked skin. She gloried in the contact, tangled her hands in his dark hair, arched her back as his lips left her mouth and descended to ignite her breasts with the same searing touch. His lips were magic, his tongue and teeth tender instruments of sorcery, and she was under their bewitching spell.

She was transported to another world, another dimension, where nothing mattered but the two of them and the shimmering halo of desire that enveloped them. She twisted beneath him, suddenly frantic with impatience to be rid of the impediment of clothing. But buttons snagged, zipper stuck, tight denim refused to budge.

He laughed softly. "Let me." Gently, deftly, he tugged the jeans over her hips until she was naked beside him. He caressed the smooth curve of her hip and nibbled a blazing trail across her abdomen, wedding the caressing glide of his hand to the satin invitation of her skin.

"My turn," she whispered. With hands less deft than his, but making up for lack of expertise with eagerness, she unfastened his belt buckle and worked the denim over angular bone and taut muscle.

And when they were naked, the lamp bathed them in a soft rainbow of light that emphasized both the rose-satin femininity of her skin and the darkly masculine glint of his chest hair.

"I could look at you forever," he murmured, his eyes roving over her possessively. "Look and touch and love . . ."

He touched each breast with his lips, then ignited her mouth again as he rolled over her and claimed her body with the masterful thrust of his own. Their bodies fit together as if the union had been measured and prophesied in eons past, and only now were their hearts and flesh and souls realizing their foretold destiny.

"We're lovers," he whispered with fierce tenderness. The thrust of his body was stilled as he held her in motionless possession. "We're lovers in the true sense of the word, because we *love*, because we are joined in more than body."

His mouth claimed hers again, but it was a claim against that which was willingly given. She met him halfway, lifting her mouth to meet his, moving her body in unison with his, pausing with him on the dreamy plateaus. There were wordless murmurs, and murmured words. There was the giving of herself and the taking of him. There was the slick, sleek feel of skin against skin, the deeper sensation of tender femininity meeting hard masculinity, and beyond the physical union was the joining of the essential core of their beings roving somewhere in lonely time and space . . . and now they had found each other.

*"Reva,"* he whispered. It was a plea, a command, an invocation.

Her lips formed his name, but no sound came. She was climbing a mountain, not struggling, but giving each ounce of herself to the climb. He was climbing with her and they were together, and then they reached the peak, the glorious peak, where they became totally one, fused with the mountain and the exploding stars. Sweet explosion that created union rather than destroyed it. Joyous upheaval, glorious blossoming that held them at the peak for long moments of rapture.

And then there was the slow, swirling glide down the far side of the mountain, gentle as a drifting feather on a gossamer cloud.

"Reva, sweet Reva," Drake whispered, holding her close, loath to reach the bottom of the mountain where mere mortals dwelt.

They lay side by side, the blanket long since tossed aside, unnecessary in the vital warmth of their own living, striving bodies. Now Drake pulled the blanket over them, tucking the corners around Reva with protective concern. Reva still drifted on her tranquil cloud, warm, damp, languid with fulfillment, still a little out of touch with reality. Her head rested on the warm, living pillow of his shoulder, and they lay without speaking, without moving, for long minutes of pure golden togetherness.

Finally Drake stirred. He touched her chin with his fingers, tilting her face up to his. "You see?" he said softly. "We're lovers. Perfect lovers. You belong to me. I belong to you."

But she was more than Drake's lover, she thought, feeling a devastating fissure in the drifting cloud of tranquility. She was Brian's mother. She took a sudden, sickening plunge into raw reality. She had been lifted, transported, transformed in Drake's passionate lovemaking. She had climbed a mystical mountain and shared a physical rapture that soared into the spiritual.

But it didn't change anything in the harsh world of reality!

Her duties and responsibilities were still there, implacable and inescapable. She couldn't selfishly think only of her own desires. Drake might be the perfect lover for her, but he was hardly the perfect father for her son.

Drake shifted on the bed and brushed a damp lock of hair from her forehead. "We have plans to make, sweet lover," he whispered.

"The plans are already made." Her voice was wooden. "I'm going to marry Mark."

# Chapter Ten

DRAKE STORMED AND stalked the room like some enraged
animal. He shouted and threatened, pleaded and demanded.
He was by turns disbelieving, angry, incredulous. He seared
her with scorn, railed at her stubbornness, blasted her mis-
guided sacrifice.

Through it all, Reva remained silent, numb. She was
beyond arguing or defending her position. She only knew
what she had to do to fulfill her duties and responsibilities.

Finally Drake stormed out, his supply of angry words
battered from contact with the blank wall of her resistance.
Though Reva had said little, she felt drained and empty.
Automatically she straightened the bed and overturned chair
and dressed slowly. With Drake gone, the room was what
it had always been, a cluttered little office and storage room
instead of a magic hideaway of shared laughter and passion.
The taste of him lingered in her mouth, and the feel of him
was imprinted on her lips and skin . . . and deeper.

She must not think of that. This had been the "one last
time" she had longed for. She must let it go at that. Drake
might yet have a physical hold on her, but she was mentally,
if not yet verbally, committed to Mark. And her heart? Her
heart was a battleground, torn between desire and duty.

Somehow she managed to drive home and crawl into her cold, lonely bed. She spent a night chasing the elusive mirage of sleep, but even when sleep came it was peopled with restless dreams.

Brian came down to the store the following morning. He wanted to earn some money beyond his regular allowance, and Reva had agreed to hire him to unpack cartons, mark prices, and clean some shelves. She was pleasantly surprised at how well he did. He was growing up! He even struck a nice balance between saving part of the money toward some special athletic shoes he wanted and splurging with the rest on video games at the arcade around the corner.

Reva explained carefully that Mark would be home today but that she had a special private discussion planned with him for this evening. She half expected Brian to demand to be included, but he just asked if he could go to the movies and then stay all night with his friend Ricky.

"You always seem to be away overnight lately," Reva murmured, feeling rather guilty.

"Yeah, I guess so. But Ricky still gets homesick, so I have to stay over there instead of having him at my house." Brian sounded a little apologetic, and Reva realized he thought she was complaining because he was leaving her home alone too often. Indeed he was growing up! She smiled and tousled his hair and was grateful that he was such a good kid. With Mark solidly behind him as a father, he'd surely not go astray as all too many kids did today.

After closing the store she hurried home and threw herself into a flurry of dinner preparations. Brown the chicken, put potatoes on to simmer. The air was uncharacteristically dead and muggy, presaging a thunderstorm. She brushed a damp strand of hair from her cheek. Them she hurried on to tear lettuce for salad, mix the homemade dressing Mark liked, and brown croutons. Mark abhorred working-women short-cuts on meals. She hoped he wouldn't notice that the choc-olate cake was from the bakery. She'd planned to bake one last night, but that was before . . .

Reva jerked her mind determinedly away from all thoughts of last night.

Mark arrived promptly at six o'clock. His manner was a little stiff and wary, but he kissed her lightly, a little off-center of the mouth.

"Welcome home," Reva said brightly. "Dinner is almost ready. Did you just get into town?"

"Actually, we got in late last night, but I didn't want to bother you at the store."

A rather different attitude from Drake's, Reva thought, but she refused to dwell on the possible interpretations of the difference.

Mark was carrying a brown paper sack. For a moment Reva thought it might be a bottle of celebration champagne, but it turned out to be some fresh vegetables from Jade's grandmother's garden. Very useful and practical.

Reva thanked him and then got out the chilled bottle of champagne she had brought home from the store. This was going to be a celebration even if she had to supply all the embellishments herself.

There was a bit of awkwardness as Mark floundered through the unfamiliar process of uncorking the champagne, but finally they were settled at the dinner table. It was a little early in the evening for candlelight, but gathering thunderclouds had darkened the sky and Reva had closed the drapes to provide intimate shadows. A trio of tapered candles flickered romantically. They were just starting to eat when the phone rang. Reva excused herself and went to answer it, thinking it was probably Brian calling.

"Is he there?" Drake demanded without polite preliminaries.

"Yes." She turned her back to the dining table so Mark couldn't hear her low, ferocious words. "What do you mean by calling me now?"

"Did I catch you at an—ah—inopportune moment?" His voice was malicious.

"We're eating dinner."

"Are you going to go through with it?"

"If you mean, am I going to tell him I came to my senses and have decided to marry him—yes! I am going to go through with it." She felt a nervous dampness in her palms, a light-headed dizziness. Why was he doing this to her? Why was he dragging out the torment? "Why are you calling me? Where are you?"

"I'm at the inn. I suppose I stayed around because I couldn't believe you'd really do it. Since you are..." He broke off, leaving the sentence unfinished. Then his voice went distant, mocking. "Give my congratulations to Mark."

No noble offer from *him* to take her back if she changed her mind, she noted. A crackle of static from the approaching storm emphasized the finality of the conversation, and Drake put a final end to it by slamming down the phone.

Reva held the receiver a few moments longer. With only the impersonal hum of the dial tone in her ear, she took time to regather her composure before returning to the table. She tacked a pleasant smile on her face and returned to Mark's conversation about Jade's newfound interest in the trampoline.

After the meal, Mark said he'd prefer to wait until later for dessert. Drake might have said the same thing after a filling meal, Reva reflected, but he'd have done it with a wickedly playful leer, and they'd have kidded and teased about just what sort of "dessert" was under discussion.

But not Mark, of course. This was serious business. Sternly she berated herself for letting her mind wander off on tangents.

She straightened in her chair and made a prim tent out of her fingers. What was the best approach to this awkward situation? She had waited until now to get to the point of this meeting, knowing Mark hated to be rushed at mealtime. She had the same uncomfortable feeling she'd had when long ago she went for her first job interview. Mark leaned back in his chair, signaling he was ready. He looked as if he were preparing to hold an interview.

"I don't know quite where to begin," Reva said uneasily.

"You didn't seem to have that problem when you informed me you were flying off to spend a weekend with Drake McQuaid." Mark spoke the name as if it were a sour taste on his tongue.

"I suppose I can only say that that was one of several

mistakes I've made recently." She took a steadying breath. "But you told me then that when—if I came to my senses, you'd be willing to reconsider our—relationship."

It was an awkward, halting speech. Somehow she had expected Mark to make this easier for her, say something clichéd but understanding, such as, "Let's let bygones be bygones." Evidently, however, he intended to drag out every painful detail. Well, that was his right, of course. She certainly didn't deserve any kidglove treatment.

"Or perhaps you've changed you mind?" she asked.

He frowned slightly, intensifying the creases that had already begun to etch his forehead. "No, I haven't changed my mind. I still feel we have the potential for creating a satisfying family life for ourselves and our children."

"But how do you feel about *me* now?"

"As I pointed out before, I'm disappointed in you. But I still believe you can be an effective mother for Jade. She knows nothing about this unpleasant situation, of course." Mark's mouth was thin-lipped with disapproval.

"Is that all you see in me, a good mother for Jade?" Reva asked, vaguely troubled. She hadn't deceived herself that Mark felt some grand passionate love for her, but this statement about her being an effective mother for Jade sounded almost impersonal. The job of mother to Jade was open, and he was considering her for the position.

"You're a very attractive woman, Reva." He inspected her, not quite as if he were seeing her for the first time, but from some new and not necessarily approving perspective. "Evidently the owner of Century Development noted that also. Although you surely must have been aware that he was merely—using you."

*Using* her? Reva felt a moment of astonished outrage as a barrage of images shot across her mind. Drake yelling, teasing, arguing, cajoling, laughing, loving. Abandoning his business appointments to help her search for Brian. Bringing her coffee and rolls so she wouldn't miss breakfast. *Using* her?

But all she said was a tight, "I admitted I'd made a mistake."

"What does Brian know about all this?"

"When Brian ran away from his father's house, Drake flew me down to San Jose in his plane. Brian met Drake at that time. But I don't think Brian knows anything specific about our relationship."

Mark toyed with his coffee cup, twisting it back and forth in the saucer. Weighing. Balancing.

"Brian is very fond of you. When he ran away and couldn't contact me, he tried to call you. I'm sure you can be an effective father for him." Reva repeated the word Mark had used to describe her potential relationship with his daughter. The word was applicable, of course, but somehow it sounded so sterile.

"And our children get along satisfactorily with each other," Mark commented. The creases on his forehead were gradually loosening as he organized his thoughts methodically to bring out the positive facets of their relationship.

"Brian is very much in need of a steady, dependable male figure in his life," Reva added.

It was all very true, very logical. Yet she felt a small breath of unease. Were they falling into the same trap as the unhappily married parents who stay together "for the sake of the children"? Parents who then proceed to make their children's lives miserable because they themselves are miserable? Drake's angry warnings shot through her mind. *It isn't enough, Reva. It isn't enough . . .*

What did Drake know? He hadn't the responsibility of a child!

"We're talking about marriage then?" Mark asked. Mark was always one to make a situation absolutely clear, leaving nothing ambiguous. Solid, dependable Mark. Life with him would never be uncertain, as it had been with Bax.

Reva took a deep breath, steadying herself for the commitment. She suddenly felt foolish about the romantic setting she had arranged. Mark didn't need that. She blew out the candles and switched on a lamp. "Yes, I'm talking about marriage."

"I'm sure you realize I'd prefer that you not work outside the home, at least until the children are older."

That wasn't totally unexpected, of course, but the stated reality of it was still something of a shock. Unmarried, she had simply forged ahead without Mark's approval when she bought the store. But that sort of independent action would not be possible once they were married, of course.

"I think I can manage a house and take care of the children satisfactorily without giving up the store," Reva argued lightly. "They're growing up. And I *like* having the store."

"Where you'd still come in contact with Drake McQuaid."

"That has nothing to do with my interest in keeping the store!"

Mark had never understood that even though she had started work out of necessity, she liked the challenge of owning her own business, enjoyed the contact with people, appreciated the good feeling of accomplishment the store gave her. And she had so many plans! She loved the exhilaration of knowing the business could become whatever her hard work and talent made of it. Drake understood that— even appreciated it.

Then a new and unrelated thought occurred to her. "Are you jealous of Drake?"

"I consider jealousy a juvenile and very negative emotion."

Reva clenched her teeth as she looked at Mark's aloof, superior expression. Not for Mark the weaknesses of mere emotional mortals.

"I'm willing to forget what has happened in the past. But if you succumbed to this man's dubious charms once, it seems reasonable to assume you might succumb again in the future if you remain in contact with him."

*Dubious charms.* There was nothing dubious about Drake's charms, physical or otherwise! If it weren't for her responsibility to Brian...

She broke off the dangerous thought to say rigidly, "I have no intention of remaining in contact with him."

"That was Drake McQuaid on the phone just a few minutes ago, wasn't it? He appears rather persistent."

*We're two of a kind*, Drake had said. *We're stubborn and determined. We go after what we want.*

Yet Drake, for all his determination and stubbornness, had some almost old-fashioned basic standards. He'd made certain she was unattached before he asked her out. He wouldn't go after a married woman. She stiffly said as much to Mark now.

Mark appeared unconvinced. He made a scornful gesture downward with his hand. "You said yourself the man was a Don Juan who thought himself irresistible to women. Surely you don't trust anything he says."

"I don't doubt his word."

"Look at his shady business dealings!"

"I see nothing shady about his business dealings. My business was in the way of his plans. He tried to get rid of it, as I suppose I would have done if I were in his position. When he failed, he altered his plans to accommodate my business."

"You're defending his actions?"

Reva realized her voice had risen to an angry shrillness as she spoke. She clutched her hands under the table, struggling for control. "I'm simply . . . explaining."

"You've still never explained to me how you could let yourself become infatuated with a man of this caliber."

Reva's jaw felt stiff. "What do you mean, a 'man of this caliber'?"

Mark shrugged, his mouth twisted disdainfully. "Woman chaser."

Reva gritted her teeth. She must control herself. Mark no doubt had a right to get in a few nasty cracks about Drake.

"Drake is very attractive to women," she said carefully. "But I don't know that he's any more of a woman chaser than any other normal man."

"I saw him, you know. I made a point of it. All good looks and flashy, phony charm. Throwing his money around up there at the inn."

"He's more than good looks! And he's not phony. He's considerate and loving and fun and hard-working—and he doesn't throw his money around. But he isn't stingy either!"

"You sound as if you're still infatuated."

"I love him!"

They stared at each other, the words hanging between them as if carved in crystal. It was true, Reva thought in mixed wonderment and dismay. She hadn't dared to admit it even to herself, but it was true.

After a long, tense silence, Mark finally said, "You don't mean that. I'm willing to forget you said it. You're just feeling defensive and guilty about being taken in by a man of that type."

Defensive? Yes. Because she loved Drake. Guilty? No!

A savage retort rose to her lips, but she bit it off. Duties, she reminded herself grimly. Responsibilities. She must not let her temper and impossible feelings for Drake ruin everything now. Brian needed a solid, reliable father.

*But I need someone too,* some other part of her echoed in anguish. A husband . . . mate . . . lover! Not this cold-eyed person whose solidity was flint-hard and glacial. There was something chilling about Mark's statement that he would forget her startling shout of love for another man, something far more frightening than all of Drake's fiery rage. Because Drake was alive, reachable, capable of love and fury, and Mark's emotions were frozen in cold, thoughtful judgment and harsh weighing of balances. He needed Reva as a mother for his daughter. He weighed that against her fall from grace and found she could still be useful. But what would they have after the children were grown and gone? In sudden panic, Reva asked herself the same question Drake had asked. And the answer was nothing. *Nothing.*

She had assured herself that life with Mark would be solid and stable, but without love the solidity was a shallow illusion. Life with Mark would be no more solid than that glittering pathway of sunlight across the sea, and she would sink in marriage to him as surely as she would sink in cold waters if she tried to walk that shiny path of illusion. She and Mark would both flounder and perhaps even drag the children into the depths of unhappiness with them.

Because without love there was no true solidity, no stability. There was nothing. Better to have no man at all, to raise Brian alone, than to marry a man she didn't love for Brian's sake. She might, heaven help her, eventually wind up *resenting* Brian if she made this sacrifice for him. Because sacrifice it was. Sacrifice. Mistake. Colossal disaster. She had been looking for a man who was the total opposite of Bax's irresponsiblity and in Mark she had found him. But she had failed to look further, to all the reasons she and Mark were disastrously wrong for each other. He would smother her with his stuffy, cautious, stolid ways; she would drive him crazy with her streaks of independence, ambition, and recklessness. There was so much of herself she had kept hidden from him, knowing he would disapprove. The playful part of her that loved teasing and laughter, the sensitive part that enjoyed quiet walks on the beach, the ambitious part that reached for success and was willing to take a few chances, the passionate part that reveled in abandoned lovemaking—all the hidden parts that Drake sought out and encouraged, because he knew she was a woman as well as a mother.

"I'm trying to be fair," Mark said.

"I think," Reva said softly, "That I have just come to my senses."

Mark studied her, his mouth slanted disapprovingly. "I take it you mean something rather different by that phrase than I did when I spoke it."

Reva nodded. "Quite different. I really do love him," she added with gentle finality.

He looked at her as if from a distance far greater than the other side of the table, as if across an enormous gulf he had never before realized existed. "This has helped me reach a decision I've been mulling over for some time," he said. He rose stiffly. "I'm going to accept a teaching position I've been offered in Seattle."

Reva knew a poignant moment of regret. She'd miss Jade, who had become almost a daughter to her and so often reminded her of her own vulnerable self of long ago. And Brian would surely miss Mark too, at least for a while.

But better a temporary loss than permanent disaster.

Mark neither stalked nor stormed out. He said polite good-byes, although a cold hostility loomed behind the controlled words.

Not a *bad* person, Reva thought as she lifted an edge of the drape and watched him walk to his car, his shoulders hunched against the rising wind and storm-mottled sky. Probably not even as emotionless and unfeeling as she had momentarily thought him to be. A good husband—for some other woman. But all Reva felt was an enormous sense of relief, as if a crushing load she had been carrying was now lifted from her. Stark, cruel jabs of lightning stabbed the sky behind his departing car. She dropped the drape and turned back to the room.

She loved Drake. The truth she had kept hidden flooded her like spring sunlight coming out from behind storm clouds. And she had sent him away!

She flew to the telephone and dialed the inn's number, uncertain what she intended to do or say but knowing she had to reach him. "Mr. McQuaid's room, please."

"I'm sorry, but Mr. McQuaid checked out a short time ago."

"Oh! Do you know where he went? Was he on his way back to Portland?"

"I'm afraid I have no idea."

Reva dashed to the window again. Wind bent the neighbor's azalea bushes over the property-line fence and rattled the screen door on the back porch. Surely Drake wouldn't try to take off and fly with this storm approaching.

Yes, he would! She knew it. Furious and frustrated with her, he'd throw his things together and head for the little airfield. She had a sudden, horrifying mental vision of the sleek plane tossed and flung to earth by the marauding strength of the storm.

She ran for her car, unmindful of wind tossing her hair and billowing her skirt. Thunder rumbled overhead as she drove north out of town toward the airfield. Fir and cedar waved and clashed in the wind, menacing shadows against brilliant flares of lightning.

Perhaps he had already taken off and was safely on his

way to Portland ahead of the storm. She could reach him there and straighten out everything. Or perhaps he was still at the airfield, waiting out the storm.

She pulled into the parking area behind the fence guarding the runway, and her heart sank as she realized that neither hopeful thought was true. The blue-and-white plane was just taxiing to the far end of the runway, making the final turn before roaring down the narrow strip.

Frantically she blinked her headlights, trying to attract his attention. There was no other activity at the little airport—none! The office was dark; all the other private planes were securely tied down or hangared. The wind socks were full and stiff. To the east, a strip of blue sky promised safety, but here storm clouds blotted the sky and lightning flickered relentlessly closer. Frantically she blinked the lights again. Surely he wouldn't . . .

The plane sped down the runway, faltered a little as it lifted off and was caught by the wind, then righted and climbed beyond the dark clump of trees at the far end of the runway. Reva got out of the car and watched the dark outline and winking lights climb, apprehension tugging inside her. Was he so furious with her that he didn't see, or wouldn't acknowledge the danger in the storm?

She realized her arms were waving frantically, uselessly, and they dropped to her sides. There was a finality about the departing plane, as there had been in Drake's mocking words on the phone. He didn't give second chances.

She could only pray that the storm wouldn't be as unyielding and unforgiving.

The winking lights curved in the prescribed takeoff pattern overhead, steady in spite of the wind. But something was wrong. The plane wasn't heading off to the northeast toward Portland. It was circling the field, descending instead of rising. Dear God, was the engine . . . ?

No. Faintly she caught the roar of the engine between the rumbles of thunder. The plane was returning. He had seen her frantic signals!

She raced along the fence, fumbled through the latched gateway, and ran a few steps, screaming Drake's name at the wind. The plane touched down, the smooth landing in the uneven wind a credit to Drake's unerring touch on the controls. She watched as the plane slowed, turned, and finally rolled to a stop as Drake guided it expertly into position between tie downs. The whirl of propeller died, and Drake climbed out and dashed to secure the tie-down lines. Reva had the bewildering feeling that he was oblivious to her presence. Or didn't care.

He had returned not because of her blinking lights but because of the storm, prudent good sense finally overriding his fury.

She should just turn and go . . .

No! She would not! She would tell him she loved him, shout it at him if she had to. We're two of a kind, he'd said. Stubborn and determined.

Rain pelted her face as she ran toward the plane, screaming his name over the gusting wind. Finally he looked up, gave a jerk of astonishment, and then strode toward her.

"What the hell are you doing here?"

"Didn't you see me? I blinked the car lights."

"I didn't see you. I was too busy trying to get the plane off the ground without losing a wing or two."

"You're an idiot, you know, taking off in weather like this just because you're angry with me!"

"You came all the way out here in this storm just to tell me I'm an idiot?" He was shouting to be heard above the wind, but she had the feeling he'd be shouting at her even if there were no storm.

"I came out here to tell you I—"

But the words *love you* were lost in a crash of thunder that shuddered the ground beneath them. Drake grabbed her arm and propelled her toward the hangar where the tall wall and a narrow roof-overhang gave some protection from the storm. Rain stung Reva's half-closed eyes and wind did a devil-dance through her hair.

"What are you doing here?" he demanded. In the shelter of the hangar wall, the wind was a notch less fierce.

"Did you turn back because of the storm?"

"Where's Crossman?"

"Someone has to answer questions. We can't just keep asking them!"

He glared down at her. His body was at right angles with the hangar wall, forming a protective niche for her. "It occurred to me there was one thing I probably hadn't told you yet. And I decided I was going to come back and say it even if I had to shove Mark Crossman out of your bed to do it."

"Say what?"

"I've said a lot of things, Reva. I said we're lovers. I said I wanted to marry you. I said you were a fool for marrying for anything but love."

"What didn't you say?"

"I love you!"

"Was it so difficult to say?" Reva asked, challenging.

"I love you, I love you, I love you! No, it isn't difficult to say." He pulled her into his arms, his touch rough but his voice as tender as the storm would allow. "I do, Reva, with all my heart. I know I don't fit your neat little mold of exactly what a father should be, but good fathers come in more than one model. And I'd do my damnedest, Reva, if you'd just give me a chance."

"How soon?" she asked recklessly.

"How soon what?"

"How soon do you want the chance? The storm will pass by morning. We could fly to Reno and be married first thing Monday morning."

He held her a few inches away to stare down into her eyes. "I think you're high on something."

"Only on love!"

He laughed then, threw back his head and laughed and picked her up and whirled her around in the wind and rain. Then he plunked her down and looked at her accusingly. "Sometimes I think you have wilder ideas than I do."

"Patience isn't one of my strong points," she agreed with a rueful smile.

"Reva, Reva, I love you so much." He buried his face in her disheveled hair. "There's nothing I'd like more than to marry you this very minute. But I don't want to do this on the spur of the moment. I want everything to be right. I want a church and a minister. I want Brian at the ceremony so he'll know how important this is to both of us, and so he'll be a part of it too."

Reva caught her breath, moved by the depth of emotion in his voice. "We'll do it right then," she told him, "with all the conventions and trimmings. We'll have an enormous cake and punch, and I'll invite my parents."

"I'll invite mine." He grinned a little wickedly. "And *then* we'll fly off by ourselves on a honeymoon."

"I have a business to run," she warned.

"So do I," he agreed without argument. A successful working wife was no threat to Drake. "And we *both* have a son to raise. But I think I could work a brother or sister or two for Brian into my busy schedule. How about you?"

"I think I could be persuaded." Her eyes danced at him. "And I'm sure you'll figure out just how to persuade me."

Then, his arm around her, they leaned into the driving rain and made their way to the car, neither of them conscious of the storm as much as they were of each other. Already a lighter strip of blue was showing on the western horizon, like a bright and shining prophecy.

For in Drake, Reva knew she had a father for her son— and more. Much, much more. For they were a man and woman who shared laughter as well as passion, companionship as well as sex. Drake was man enough to accept her work and ambitions. With him, she could be all the parts of the woman she was: wife, mother, lover, friend. Together they could be explorers in love, parents to Brian and perhaps to other children who might follow.

And always and forever, lovers.

____ 06540-4 **FROM THE TORRID PAST #49** Ann Cristy
____ 06544-7 **RECKLESS LONGING #50** Daisy Logan
____ 05851-3 **LOVE'S MASQUERADE #51** Lillian Marsh
____ 06148-4 **THE STEELE HEART #52** Jocelyn Day
____ 06422-X **UNTAMED DESIRE #53** Beth Brookes
____ 06651-6 **VENUS RISING #54** Michelle Roland
____ 06595-1 **SWEET VICTORY #55** Jena Hunt
____ 06575-7 **TOO NEAR THE SUN #56** Aimée Duvall
____ 05625-1 **MOURNING BRIDE #57** Lucia Curzon
____ 06411-4 **THE GOLDEN TOUCH #58** Robin James
____ 06596-X **EMBRACED BY DESTINY #59** Simone Hadary
____ 06660-5 **TORN ASUNDER #60** Ann Cristy
____ 06573-0 **MIRAGE #61** Margie Michaels
____ 06650-8 **ON WINGS OF MAGIC #62** Susanna Collins
____ 05816-5 **DOUBLE DECEPTION #63** Amanda Troy
____ 06675-3 **APOLLO'S DREAM #64** Claire Evans
____ 06680-X **THE ROGUE'S LADY #69** Anne Devon
____ 06689-3 **SWEETER THAN WINE #78** Jena Hunt
____ 06690-7 **SAVAGE EDEN #79** Diane Crawford
____ 06692-3 **THE WAYWARD WIDOW #81** Anne Mayfield
____ 06693-1 **TARNISHED RAINBOW #82** Jocelyn Day
____ 06694-X **STARLIT SEDUCTION #83** Anne Reed
____ 06695-8 **LOVER IN BLUE #84** Aimée Duvall

All of the above titles are $1.75 per copy

---

*Available at your local bookstore or return this form to:*

**SECOND CHANCE AT LOVE**
*Book Mailing Service*
*P.O. Box 690, Rockville Centre, NY 11571*

Please send me the titles checked above. I enclose _____
Include $1.00 for postage and handling if one book is ordered; 50¢ per book for
two or more. California, Illinois, New York and Tennessee residents please add
sales tax.

NAME _____

ADDRESS _____

CITY _____ STATE/ZIP _____
(allow six weeks for delivery)                          SK-41b

All of the above titles are $1.75 per copy except where noted

_____ 07201-X **RESTLESS TIDES** #113 Kelly Adams $1.95
_____ 07202-8 **MOONLIGHT PERSUASION** #114 Sharon Stone $1.95
_____ 07203-6 **COME WINTER'S END** #115 Claire Evans $1.95
_____ 07204-4 **LET PASSION SOAR** #116 Sherry Carr $1.95
_____ 07205-2 **LONDON FROLIC** #117 Josephine Janes $1.95
_____ 07206-0 **IMPRISONED HEART** #118 Jasmine Craig $1.95
_____ 07207-9 **THE MAN FROM TENNESSEE** #119 Jeanne Grant $1.95
_____ 07208-7 **LAUGH WITH ME, LOVE WITH ME** #120 Lee Damon $1.95
_____ 07209-5 **PLAY IT BY HEART** #121 Vanessa Valcour $1.95
_____ 07210-9 **SWEET ABANDON** #122 Diana Mars $1.95
_____ 07211-7 **THE DASHING GUARDIAN** #123 Lucia Curzon $1.95
_____ 07212-5 **SONG FOR A LIFETIME** #124 Mary Haskell $1.95
_____ 07213-3 **HIDDEN DREAMS** #125 Johanna Phillips $1.95
_____ 07214-1 **LONGING UNVEILED** #126 Meredith Kingston $1.95
_____ 07215-X **JADE TIDE** #127 Jena Hunt $1.95
_____ 07216-8 **THE MARRYING KIND** #128 Jocelyn Day $1.95
_____ 07217-6 **CONQUERING EMBRACE** #129 Ariel Tierney $1.95

---

*Available at your local bookstore or return this form to:*

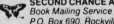 **SECOND CHANCE AT LOVE**
*Book Mailing Service*
P.O. Box 690, Rockville Centre, NY 11571

Please send me the titles checked above. I enclose _____
Include $1.00 for postage and handling if one book is ordered; 50¢ per book for
two or more. California, Illinois, New York and Tennessee residents please add
sales tax.

NAME _____

ADDRESS _____

CITY _____ STATE/ZIP _____

(allow six weeks for delivery)

SK-41d

# WHAT READERS SAY ABOUT
# SECOND CHANCE AT LOVE BOOKS

"Your books are the greatest!"
  —*M. N., Carteret, New Jersey**

"I have been reading romance novels for quite some time, but the SECOND CHANCE AT LOVE books are the most enjoyable."
  —*P. R., Vicksburg, Mississippi**

"I enjoy SECOND CHANCE [AT LOVE] more than any books that I have read and I do read a lot."
  —*J. R., Gretna, Louisiana**

"I really think your books are exceptional . . . I read Harlequin and Silhouette and although I still like them, I'll buy your books over theirs. SECOND CHANCE [AT LOVE] is more interesting and holds your attention and imagination with a better story line . . ."
  —*J. W., Flagstaff, Arizona**

"I've read many romances, but yours take the 'cake'!"
  —*D. H., Bloomsburg, Pennsylvania**

"Have waited ten years for *good* romance books. Now I have them."
  —*M. P., Jacksonville, Florida**

*Names and addresses available upon request